The Farmhouse behind the Bakery

Kim Peterson

Fulton Books
Meadville, PA

Published by Fulton Books 2022

ISBN 979-8-88731-302-3 (paperback)
ISBN 979-8-88731-303-0 (digital)

Printed in the United States of America

Chapter 1

I didn't pack much. I didn't have much. When my dad got sick, I moved back home to help my mom take care of my dad. It wasn't the first time he was on the brink of death, but he always seemed to come back. But not really. Each time he was hospitalized, he came home a little worse off—more machines, more medicine, more sadness. It was too much for my mom, so I left the little apartment I had near the college and moved back home.

My mom and I were best friends. At night, my dad's machines were loud, so my mom would sneak out of their room and come to my bed. We would talk quietly until one of us would fall asleep or at least until the buzzer would go off on my dad's machine. Then we would both get up. Fixing the machine was a one-person job, but we would both get up to support each other. It was easier if one of us would reset the machine and the other would deal with calming down my dad.

The machine made it worse for my dad. When it would go off, it would startle him awake. He would go from just moaning to out and out screaming about how much he just wanted to die. It was terrible for my mom. My dad had gone from a strong, hard-working man to wearing diapers, being unable to get out of bed.

At the beginning, he would constantly talk about how he just couldn't wait to ride his tractor around in the summer and cut the lawn. I would constantly remind him that cutting the lawn was over-rated. Eventually, the lack of oxygen to his brain began to show its effect. He was always sharp and quick-witted, but that was taken away from him too. He was reduced to mumbling and mostly talking about things that we couldn't understand.

When my dad passed away, it was both terribly sad and a relief. I felt guilty for being relieved, but he had suffered for so long. It had been over a week since he was able to eat or drink. His throat had begun to gurgle, which was so hard for my mom to hear. The night he died, my mom and I could hear him talking to his grandma. We lay there and just listened. It was so strange. When his machine went off for the final time, we didn't jump up as we usually did. We looked at each other and just knew.

The first few months after his death were hard for my mom. For so many years, my mom's life was consumed with taking care of my dad that she almost didn't know what to do with all her free time. I tried to keep her busy going through my dad's belongings. Each day, we would pack up a little more. Before my dad faded, he had told my mom about a hidden stash of cash he had in his sock drawer. When she pulled it out after his death, she laughed about how he loved to hide money for their casino trips. Eventually, the only thing left were fond memories.

Eventually, my mom adjusted to not having to be a caretaker. She began knitting again and doing some of the things she didn't have time to do. As much as we loved each other, we both knew we had to live our own lives. I didn't want to leave her. She really didn't want me to leave either, but she wanted me to start fresh and experience life. She almost forced me out. I knew I should go, but I wasn't sure I should leave her.

I packed up my old Chevy truck and started out on a new adventure. I didn't know where I was going, but it was summer and the options were endless. I never was much of a planner. I thought I would head up north. Where up north? I didn't know. All I knew was that I wanted to spend as much time as possible near the beach. I wanted to sit on the lakeshore, soak in the sun, watch the waves, and forget about life for a while.

I'm not sure how long I have been driving. My mind was somewhere between a blank stare and completely focused. I have no idea where I was going or what I was even doing. I reached down to the cupholder and pulled a ponytail holder out. Reaching up, I grabbed my hair and put it in a bun on top of my head. Grabbing the red bandanna that hung from my rearview mirror, I tied it around my head. "I can do it!" I whispered to myself as I looked in the mirror, thinking I looked like Rosie the Riveter. I opened the windows to feel the sun and fresh air on my face.

I glance down at the clock. I've already been on the road for a couple of hours. I should call my mom. It is weird to be alone. I miss her already. It has been quite some time since I haven't had her by my side. We have grown closer in the last few months than ever before. We had talked about everything. We were each other's support. My thoughts of the past year started to consume me, and my eyes filled up with tears. I rolled down the window the rest of the way and turned on the music just loud enough to block out my thoughts. I decided I should probably make a pit stop to fill up with gas, take care of my craving for some gas station beef jerky, and call my mom.

Taking my hoop earrings out, I tried calling my mom. She didn't answer. I know I had no right, but I was kind of irritated that she wasn't just waiting around for my call. Putting my earrings back in, I finished up the bag of jerky and sipped on the piping hot cup of coffee. How a coffee can burn the top of my mouth after adding three creamers, I don't understand. I debated in my head if I could sue them, like the old lady that spilled coffee on her crotch and then sued McDonalds. Putting the key in the ignition, I tried to start the truck. Although it started, it seemed to take a little longer than what it was supposed to. Not being a mechanic, I decided just ignoring the problem was the best option and started back on the expressway.

With the windows down, my hair tied up, and the music playing, I felt good. I reviewed my life in my head. After quitting college and getting an apartment, I was kind of at a standstill. I knew college wasn't for me. I also knew that working in an office every day wasn't for me either. Sitting at a reception desk and answering the phones wasn't hard work. Some people would probably consider it the ideal job. I got decent pay for answering phones and watching TikToks on my phone all day, but the boredom was killing me. Some days, the thought of going into work almost made me sick. I would dream of getting in a car crash just so I wouldn't have to go in. I didn't want to die, but I thought a good broken arm or leg could maybe justify at least six weeks off. When things got worse for my dad, I jumped at the opportunity to move back home to help my mom.

Now that my mom was doing okay and considering the fact that I had no job and no place to live, the opportunity seemed like the best time to start this new adventure. I considered traveling overseas, maybe to Italy, but the realization that my bank account was small put that thought to an end. I also wanted to be close enough to home that if my mom needed me, I could be there for her. I knew I could afford to spend the summer on the road before I would have to get another job and get back to reality. I wanted to visit every small town along the way up north—the kind of town where everyone knows everyone else, where old people sit on their front porch and drink coffee and gossip about neighbors, where everyone sat on lawn chairs in their backyard around a firepit, drinking beer and laughing, where you would get up on Sunday morning and cook pancake breakfast for your family before heading to church.

Looking down, I saw a light on my dash that wasn't there before. Now how was I supposed to know what that was a picture of? I was guessing it was an engine, but it looked more like a fat helicopter to me. I am not sure how long it had been on, but I am sure it had something to do with the slow start at the gas station. Well that can't be good. Maybe if I just ignored it, it would go back off. Plus, if it was a real emergency, I think it would be a picture of fire or maybe a skull and crossbones. I looked over to the passenger seat to see if there was anything to cover it up with. I decided an empty Splenda packet from my coffee should work. I tucked the bottom of the wrapper in between the glass and the dashboard. It worked perfectly. It's like I fixed the problem. Mental note: I would check to see if there was a repair shop at the next exit that could look at it.

As the day was coming to a close, I wondered why all the cars started passing me. I pushed down on the accelerator, and nothing happened. It seemed like my truck wasn't switching gears. I turned down the radio to help me concentrate. The grinding, buzzing noise couldn't be good. As more lights came on the dash, I reached down and removed the Splenda packet. My speed decreased from crawling to a stop. I turned on my fourways and pulled off to the side of the road. There had to be an exit coming up soon. I pulled out my phone to check Google Maps to see how far it was to the next exit.

Just over a mile seemed close enough to walk, but I wasn't sure what was even at the next exit. I had to think. Thank God my dad wasn't around to see this. I would have had to listen to him lecturing me on how I should have taken my truck to have a "once-over" before I left. I did change the oil and fill up the windshield washer fluid. Who would have known this would happen? More important now was how I was going to get to the next exit. *Should I call a tow truck? How am I even going to pay for the fix? I budgeted just enough money to get me through the summer.* I was glad that my mom had given me a little of my dad's casino cash. I would definitely need it now. *Oh please, dear God, I need help.*

Just as that prayer passed over my lips, a white truck pulled up behind me. I looked in the rearview mirror to see if I could see who was driving. All I could see was that it was a man with a baseball hat on and a black T-shirt. It was hard to make out his features through his front window, although he looked to be a little older than me. I glanced in the mirror to see how bad I looked. I decided that my Rosie the Riveter look seemed less likely to be able to do anything now. I watched as he got out of his truck and headed toward the driver's side. At a quick glance, it didn't look as though he had any weapons on him, although a knife or handgun could easily be hidden. I had watched enough *Datelines* to know this could be the end for me, and being murdered would surely ruin this trip.

Rolling down the window all the way, I looked at him, and words just spewed out of my mouth. "The check engine light came on a few miles back," I lied, not wanting him to think I was an idiot that covered up the light with a Splenda packet. "I was trying to make it to the next exit to see if I could get help."

He nodded his head and placed his hands on the door, where the window was rolled down. They were thick hands, working-man hands. This wasn't a guy that worked in the office every day, drank coffee, and wrote reports. He worked hard for a living. He was just the kind of man I needed for this situation. Looking directly at me, he had a thick crease between his eyes, probably from squinting in the sun all day. "What was it doing?"

"It just kind of stopped doing anything. I pushed on the gas, and it wouldn't switch gears. It wouldn't accelerate. The RPMs just started jumping up and then going down. Do you know if there is any place I could take it nearby?"

"Yes. Pete's Auto Repair is at the next exit. Let me pull my truck in front of yours. I have a strap that I can hook up, and we can tow it there." He didn't really give me the option as he walked back to his truck and moved it in front of mine. I wasn't sure if I should sit in my truck or get out. I decided I would get out and watch him. I felt less helpless this way.

He jumped out of his truck and opened the back door as he reached for something. Walking back with the yellow strap, he threw it on the ground and crawled under the front of my truck. "I am going to have to hook it to the frame." He had obviously done this before.

I crouched down and tried to pretend that I understood what he was saying. He lay on his side, and his legs stuck out from underneath my truck. His Levi jeans were worn and covered his dark brown cowboy boots. They weren't the pointed-toed boots, but the round-toed ones. It looked like they might have been steel toed. I wondered if he was a construction worker. I would have asked, but he wasn't much for small talk. He was all business.

Climbing out, he said, "Okay, are you ready?"

"Ready for what?" I asked.

"To tow your truck to Pete's," he responded.

"Um. Not really. I have no idea what I need to do." I began to panic. This wasn't anything I had ever had to do before.

His goatee turned up around his mouth, with a slight smirk. He looked at me sideways. He explained everything I needed to do. I tried to commit it to memory. Put the car in neutral. He would tap his brake lights when we needed to slow down so I could stop both his truck and mine. Most importantly, keep the tow strap tight. It all seemed like a lot to remember, but I jumped in the driver's seat and tried to remember everything.

The two-mile trip to Pete's was the most stressful thing I had done in a while. When we arrived, he jumped out of his truck and walked back to me. "Put it in park," he said as he disappeared back under the front of my truck and unhooked his strap. Then he threw it in his truck bed and waited for me to get out.

"Thanks so much. I don't know what I would have done if you hadn't come along. That was super stressful." My hands were still shaking.

"You did fine," he said matter-of-factly, continuing with his to-the-point demeanor. I felt as if I did better than fine; hopefully, I will never have to do it again.

He led the way to the building and pushed on the dirty glass window that simply stated, "Pete's." The bell rang, and he walked in. I followed behind. A small-statured man came around the corner from where I imagined he was working on another vehicle, wiping his hands with an oily shop rag. He was dark-skinned, and I would guess he was in his early seventies. His nametag on this blue mechanic's jumpsuit said, "Pedro."

"Hi, Pete, this is…I guess I don't know your name," he laughed.

"I'm Melissa." I jumped in. I could feel my cheeks becoming red. He looked at me and smirked again.

"I'm Chris." He continued, "I think Mel's truck might have a bad transmission. She broke down on the expressway. Do you think you would be able to help her out?" I tried to ignore the fact that he called me Mel. My dad was the only person that ever called me Mel. I liked the way he said it, though.

"I should be able to take a look at it, but I won't be able to do anything for a few days." He looked at Chris and then at me. "Would that work for you?"

"Unfortunately, I don't really have any other option. Are there any hotels or motels around here that I could stay at?"

Chris jumped in and spoke directly to Pedro. "I'll take her over to the Johnson Farm. It's still vacant." Pedro wrote down my number and told me he would call and let me know as soon as he knew something. I followed Chris out to his truck. He opened my door, and I jumped in. This was the first time a man had ever opened a door for me.

"Kathy is the owner of the Johnson Farm. It's the old farm on the west side of the road that we passed on the way to Pete's. She rents the farmhouse that sits behind her bakery and farmstand. The bakery is only open until six, but we can swing over to her house to see if you could stay there."

We continued the rest of the way in silence. The day's events were running through my head. How would I even be able to pay for a new transmission? How much would it cost to rent a farmhouse for a few days? I considered the idea of sleeping in the back of my truck. If it was just going to be in Pete's parking lot, I could just blow up the air mattress that I planned on using at a campground. I was afraid my adventure was already over.

"We're here," Chris interrupted my thoughts. "I've known Kathy my whole life. She went to school with my parents." We pulled up the long dirt driveway, and Chris got out. Once again, I followed him up to the door. This was starting to be a habit, but I had to admit that he looked good from behind.

An older woman answered the door and invited us inside. I let Chris do all the talking. She looked at me sympathetically and put her hand on my shoulder. Kathy walked back to the kitchen and opened what looked to be a junk drawer. Pulling out a set of keys, she put them in my hands. "Does $30 a week work?"

"That would be great. I can't thank you enough." I exhaled a sigh of relief. At that cost, it was cheaper than staying in a campground and way better than sleeping in the back of my truck.

"No problem, honey. Stop by the bakery in the morning, and I can fill you in on some quirks with the old farmhouse. Plus you can get one of my famous doughnuts." She hugged me goodbye as if I was an old friend.

As we headed back to Chris's truck, he asked, "Are you hungry?"

"No, I think I would like to just go get settled in for the night. Would you mind just swinging by Pete's? I totally forgot to grab my clothes." He nodded, again, keeping it simple.

After getting my duffle bag, we drove back to the farmhouse in silence. Chris reached across my lap and opened the glove box. As his arm brushed my leg, I could feel my face heat up. He grabbed a pen and a pad of paper. He wrote down his phone number and handed it to me. "I live right up the street. If you need anything in the next couple of days, don't hesitate to give me a call."

"I can't thank you enough for everything today." I wasn't sure if I should shake his hand or give him a hug, so I just jumped out and walked toward the front door. A sensor light came on, and I could see that Chris was waiting to make sure I was in the house before he left. I opened the door and looked for a light to flip on before I shut the door. Flipping it on, I looked back and waved. As the truck left the driveway, I shut the door and decided it was a good time to try and call my mom again.

Chapter 2

A bright light turned on in the distance and shone through the bedroom window. Upon opening my eyes, I woke up confused, Where was I? Picking up my phone, I checked the time, 3:00 am. I walked over to the window and looked out just in time to see Kathy walking into her bakery. Lying back in bed, I thought about my first day. Although it didn't really go as planned, at least, I had a nice bed to stay in and could get a fresh doughnut in the morning.

I lay in bed as long as I could. I never really fell back to sleep. Thoughts of my mom, my poor truck, Chris, and Kathy ran through my mind, mostly Chris though. Picking up my phone, I checked the time again, 8:00 am. I decided to get my day started. I needed to make some kind of plan for the day. The first thing I needed to do was walk over to the bakery and talk to Kathy. I prayed the bakery had coffee.

Walking out the front door, I noticed an old wooden swing on the front porch that I hadn't seen the night before. It looked like it had seen better days, but the chains that were hooked on either side of the swing and attached to the top of the porch seemed sturdy enough to hold a few people. Leaning against the wall behind it was an old green Schwinn bicycle with a basket. If I got the okay to use it from Kathy, I would try out both the swing and the bike this afternoon. Cutting through the edge of the field, I headed straight to the bakery.

I walked into the old red pole barn that was at some point converted to a bakery. The front was filled with fresh-baked goods, homemade jams, dried soup mixes, and some fresh fruit and vegetables. Behind the doughnut counter and through a glass wall, I could see Kathy next to a gigantic mixer and a large wooden table covered with flour. "Can I help you?" a young woman asked from behind the doughnut case.

"Um yes, can I get one of those long john doughnuts that are filled with the white cream?" Handing it to me, she asked if I needed anything else. I asked her if she could see if Kathy had a second to talk. I handed her a crumpled up dollar from my pocket.

Turning around, she knocked on the glass. Looking up, Kathy held up one finger, signaling that she needed to finish what she was working on. The young woman, whom I was guessing was home for the summer from college, pointed to a red picnic table that sat right outside the front door. "You can wait for her there. She will be with you in a few minutes. Would you like a cup of coffee? It's free." She didn't wait for an answer and just handed me a small white cup. I guess she could tell the answer was yes by the way my eyes lit up. "There is cream and sugar on the table next to the coffee pot." I decided that already, the bakery was my new favorite place.

Grabbing my coffee, I headed through the front door to sit at the table. I debated if I should sit facing the parking lot or inside the building. I decided to sit facing the building so I could see when Kathy was heading toward me. I was glad I did. I watched as all the locals came in to get their fresh doughnuts. A fire truck pulled into the parking lot. As the two young men got out, I could see their yellow uniforms and guessed they were on their way back from a call. A younger crowd came in on their way to high school, which I imagined had about a month left. Some young men came in just to see the cashier. Her eyes would light up, and I could tell they were flirting with her. I wished I had propped the door open so I could eavesdrop on their conversations.

I was so into spying on them that I didn't notice Kathy walking up to the table. With coffee in hand, she sat down. "Hi, honey," she greeted me the way she did the night before. She didn't wait for me to answer. "Looks like you made it through the night okay."

"Oh I did. I am so grateful that your house was available." I looked at her as I spoke. I guessed she was probably in her early seventies, but she didn't look old. She seemed strong and fit although I could tell she carried a little extra weight under her apron. I assumed that was from eating so many of her baked goods.

"What are your plans for the week?" She didn't wait for my answer. "If you haven't noticed, there is a bike on the front porch. You can use that if you want to ride into town and get some groceries. You will probably need to blow up the tires. The pump is in the closet closest to the front door." She pointed down the road. "Just head straight down this road until you get to the light. If you go right, you will hit the grocery store and hardware store. If you go left, there is the library, a bar that has the best fish and chips special on Friday nights. It's right next to Pete's repair shop and the fire station. If you head straight through the light, the road curves around, and you will eventually hit Lake Michigan. It's about eight miles away." Standing up, she announced, "Welp, I better get back at it. Stop by anytime just to chat."

I watched her walk back into the kitchen, and I stood up to head back to the farmhouse. I decided the first thing I needed to do was to go to the store and get some supplies. I had forgotten to pack deodorant, and the day was already heating up. I needed to write a list of all the essentials that I could pack in the basket at one time.

Unlocking the front door, I beelined to the bathroom. An old bar of yellow Dial soap sat on the dish in the sink. I needed to add soap to the list, but for right now, this would work. Pulling my shirt over my head, I wet down my armpits and scrubbed away the sweat. I decided it was nice enough for a T-shirt and shorts. I threw on a baseball cap so I wouldn't get too much sun on my face. One last stop in the kitchen, I checked the cupboards to see if there were plates, glasses, silverware, and pans to use or if I would have to buy some. Before heading out the front door, I grabbed the tire pump from the closet.

After filling up the tires with air, I carried the bike down the two front steps and jumped on the seat. This was a seat made for comfort. It was cushioned and wide, perfect for cruising the roads. Crossing over the street, I headed to town. The wind was blowing just enough to keep me cool, but not hard enough to slow me down. The road was lined with farmland. Tractors were running up and down the fields. I recognized the white truck next to one wooden barn near the road. Chris. I looked off in the distance to see if I could tell if it was him on the big green tractor. It was too far to see. I would try to look again on the way home from town.

Kathy's directions led me right downtown, if you could consider it a "downtown." Businesses lined both sides of the road, and tall black light poles lined the streets. It looked like every small town you would see in a family Christmas special.

Walking into the front of the grocery store, the first thing I noticed was a counter with tall pink barstools. An old couple sat at the counter, drinking shakes. They both turned around when the bell on the door rang to see if they recognized me. Candy jars with metal scoops lined the countertop with every kind of candy you can imagine. Little bags sat next to a scale. Candy was my downfall. "Need anything?" the lady working the soda counter asked in a deep voice. I couldn't smell cigarettes, but I could tell she was a serious smoker. The old couple looked me up and down and began to whisper to each other, obviously recognizing I wasn't from around there.

The bike basket was only so big, so I settled on only getting a bag of small fireball jawbreakers and some red string licorice. Then I started walking up and down each aisle. Since I needed some groceries from the refrigerator, I wouldn't be able to stop at the library today. For now, I would pick up a magazine to look through on the swing.

The cashier was the same lady that worked at the soda counter. She raced over to the register when she saw me unload my groceries on the conveyor belt. "You new to town?" she asked. Since no one was behind me, I told her that I was renting Kathy's farmhouse and gave her the short version of how I would be around until my truck was fixed. She told me all about Pete and how he had started that shop thirty years ago. He had come into town with the rest of his family to work at some farms, but he had other ideas. He started his auto repair shop and never left.

"Pete is always willing to work with everyone. If you can't pay him right away, he will let you work out a payment plan or do some kind of work exchange with you. That is how he built up his reputation. Everyone trusts and appreciates him." That is probably why he couldn't look at my truck for a few days, I thought to myself.

She continued to fill me in on Chris. Lowering her voice, she told me he was the town's most popular bachelor although apparently he didn't show any interest in dating anyone. "Every girl in town has tried to get his attention. We all thought he was going to marry Cyndee, his high school girlfriend, but she went to college and he stayed here to work on the family farm. When she came home pregnant on Christmas break, it broke his heart. Ever since then, he has been all work and no play. Of course, that hasn't stopped single women from seventeen to seventy-five to try and win his heart." Narrowing her eyes and giving me a once-over, she warned, "So you shouldn't waste your time thinking about him again. He helped you the way he helps everyone. It's just who he is. Plus, no offense but unless you want to piss off every woman in town, I wouldn't go out of my way to see him again." Handing me back my change, she added, "I'm Connie, by the way."

Grabbing my few bags, I told her I would see her again later in the week. Loading up my bags into the basket, I looked back as Connie raced back to the soda counter. I could tell she was filling the old couple in on me. I smiled when she saw me glancing at her. She waved, and I waved back. If I ever wanted to know anything, I knew I could ask Connie.

The ride back was a lot easier with my back to the wind. I ignored Connie's warning and looked to see if Chris was out on the tractor. I really wasn't interested in him until Connie told me I shouldn't be. Unfortunately, the tractor was parked, and his truck was gone.

Chapter 3

After putting away my groceries, I walked around to every room and opened up the windows. The fresh air filled the house. I swear I could smell Lake Michigan. Then I grabbed my bag of jawbreakers, a Vernors, and the *People* magazine and headed out to the front porch. As I sat down on the porch swing, the chains creaked. Looking up, I double-checked the hooks to make sure I wouldn't crash down. I decided to lighten the load and take off my shoes and socks. The cool breeze felt nice on my feet.

With the fresh air blowing on my face, I leaned back on the swing, pushing myself back and forth slowly. Putting a fireball in my mouth, I started flipping through the magazine. I wasn't reading anything, just looking at the pictures. I love the "Who does it better?" pictures of the different stars wearing the same outfit. Taking my hand, I covered up the check mark at the bottom to see if I guessed the right picture, usually getting it wrong.

Turning sideways, I decided to lie down on the swing. The fresh air and the long bike ride started to have a toll. I could feel my eyes shutting. I was just resting my eyes, or so I thought. Suddenly I had the feeling as if someone was watching me. Opening my eyes, I popped up. "Chris, you scared me."

With his familiar smirk, he gave an insincere apology. "Oh sorry, Mel. Kathy was having an electrical issue and called to see if I could come fix it. Turns out it was just a blown fuse. When I was leaving, she asked if I could stop over to make sure you weren't having any issues with this old house."

"Where is your truck at?" I asked, looking at the driveway. "I should have heard you drive up. Want to sit down? I can grab you something to drink."

"I just decided to walk over." Sitting down, he continued, "How is the house working out? Have you heard anything from Pete yet?"

As he sat down, I suddenly felt nervous. He already told me the only reason he stopped by was because Kathy asked him to. He obviously didn't want me to be confused that he had any interest in me. Then why was my face heating up?

Trying to lower my nose without being too obvious, I tried to sniff my armpit. I still hadn't put on the deodorant. I wondered if I had BO. "The house is perfect. Thanks again. I don't know what I would have done without your help. I haven't heard anything from Pete yet. He said it would be a couple of days, so I decided I would stop in and talk to him tomorrow. I went today to get groceries but didn't get the chance to go to the library. I thought it would give me something to do tomorrow." I stopped talking when I realized I was just rattling off too much information.

Nodding, Chris listened to what I felt was me going on and on. Since he didn't talk much, I felt pressured to fill in the quietness with words. He finally asked, after what seemed to be minutes, "Did you find everything you needed at the store? It really just has the necessities. Did you meet Connie?" I nodded, and he continued, "I am sure everyone in town already knows all about you by now. They probably know things about you that you didn't even know. Word travels fast in a small town."

"Yes, she was interesting for sure." I think the fact that Chris looked so directly into my eyes is what made me so nervous. His eyes were penetrating, somewhere between light blue and gray. The thick crease between them made him look like he was always thinking, which, from what I could tell from his personality, was probably true. "Are you sure you don't want anything to drink?"

"No, thanks. I really have to get back to work." Standing up, he said, "You can call if you need anything, or just tell Kathy, and she will send me over." He grinned.

"Well Connie did warn me that I shouldn't be calling you, so I might just call Kathy instead." It was my turn to smirk. Even though his back was turned to me and he didn't acknowledge my remark, I knew he had heard me. He shook his head as he walked back across the field to his truck.

"Bye. Don't be a stranger," I yelled, rethinking if I should have said that. Rubbing my forehead with my fingers, I shook my head too.

After throwing another jawbreaker in my mouth, I just sat there enjoying the fresh air. I decided to call my mom to see how she was holding up. Surprisingly, she was doing quite well. I didn't want to, but I felt a little hurt that she was getting along so well without me. She even decided she was going to get a volunteer job at the mission store in town. She thought it would keep her busy, and all the volunteers were in their late sixties or early seventies. She thought she would like to be with people at the same stage in life as her.

With the day coming to an end, I thought I would take a walk. Instead of heading into town, I headed in the opposite direction. I turned onto the first dirt road I came to to see where it would lead me. Being directionally challenged, I didn't want to head too far from my place. Checking my phone, I double-checked to see if I had service this far out in the country. As I came up on the next road, I decided to turn around and head back. The cows at the corner ranch watched me as I crossed over, running toward the fence. "Hi," I greeted them, snapping a picture to send to my mom. I wanted to go up and pet their noses, but I didn't know if that was even a thing you did with cows. Plus, I didn't know if they would bite my fingers off. I decided just to stick with a picture for now.

Once back, I jumped in the shower and decided to make myself a grilled cheese and tomato sandwich. It hit the spot. I only wished I had bought some Jose Cuervo. I would pick some up in town tomorrow, I decided. Thinking to myself, I wondered if Connie would let everyone know I was a drinker. Sitting down, I flipped on the TV. I decided to watch *Jeopardy*. A terrible habit I formed from staying with my mom, by eight o'clock, I was ready for bed. The fresh air and exercise had taken their toll on me.

Chapter 4

Waking up early, I decided to make a plan for the day before I even got out of bed. With the thick homemade quilt wrapped tightly around me, I snuggled in tighter. I could feel the wind coming through the window. I breathed in the fresh country air. Thinking over the smell, I wondered if I could smell Kathy's fresh doughnuts. Nope, it was just cows. Shutting my eyes, I decided to go back to sleep for a little while longer.

Heading down to the kitchen, I realized I bought coffee but no filters. Ugh! "Filters and tequila," I needed to write down my new list. Opening up all the drawers, there had to be something I could write on. Reaching into my pocket, I pulled out the scrap of paper with Chris's phone number. After setting it on the counter, I decided not to use that paper. My thoughts wondered about Chris and what he was really thinking about me—probably nothing. I wasn't really sure if I was thinking anything about him yet either. I would just keep a mental grocery list. I decided to start my day with a walk to the bakery for a doughnut and a free cup of coffee.

As I entered the bakery, the young girl wasn't standing behind the counter. Instead, Kathy stood there. "Hi, Melissa," she greeted me. "Did Chris stop by to see you yesterday?"

"Yes. He didn't stay long though. He isn't much of a talker. He said he was able to fix your electrical problem yesterday."

Kathy looked me in the eyes and smiled, "Oh, honey, I didn't really have an electrical problem. I flipped the switch in the fuse box and used it as an excuse to get Chris here. You know he's single, right? That's why I sent him over to see you. I knew he would come right away if I told him there was an electrical problem. You know, we can't risk this place burning down." She winked at me and continued,

"Ever since my husband died, he has been my guardian angel. He is like a son to me. There isn't anyone in this town that is good enough for Chris, and he has been single long enough. I thought maybe I could work as a matchmaker and try to fix him up with my new favorite tenant. What can I get you?"

Hmmm, Kathy was sneaky and devious. I liked that about her. Plus, she smelled like doughnuts. Maybe no one in this town was good enough for her either. I wondered how long ago her husband had died. Maybe I would scope out the town and see if there was someone I could find for her. I guess it really just depended on how long it would take Pete to fix my truck. I might be gone before the end of the week. "I'll take another one of those amazing long johns. I really need some coffee too."

She handed me the bag, and I handed her my money. Pointing to the pot of coffee, she announced, "You know where it's at." Then she added, "Let me know if it's not hot enough. I might be having more electrical issues again."

I turned around quickly, and she was laughing. "I did mention that Chris is single, right?"

"Yeah, I may have heard that before, although you should know that Connie warned me to stay away from him for my own good."

"Connie is a busybody. She should just worry about finding herself a good man, not the losers she usually dates. Maybe if she didn't talk about everyone behind their backs, she would bring in a higher quality of man for herself. You just worry about Chris, that handsome, hard-working, kind, thoughtful man. I will take care of the people in this town, especially the people that should be minding their own business."

Waving goodbye, I headed out the door and back home. Stopping at the porch swing, I decided not to even go inside. Reaching into the bag, I pulled out the doughnut. I probably shouldn't make a habit of eating doughnuts every day. Licking the chocolate off my knuckles, I decided that I could have worse habits than eating doughnuts, like smoking—smoking like Connie does. Thinking about Connie, I decided I agreed with Kathy—she should mind her own business.

Crumpling up the bag, I walked inside and glanced into the refrigerator. What would I have for dinner tonight? I wish I had looked before I ate the doughnut. If I were hungry, maybe I would have better ideas of what I could eat. Instead, I just shut the refrigerator door and grabbed my old baseball cap off the counter. Pulling my ponytail through the hole, I pulled the rim over my forehead. Squeezing the bill to round my face, I headed out the front door and grabbed the bike.

Pedaling down the road, the wind felt refreshing. Letting my mind travel to Lake Michigan, I wondered if the wind came off of the lake. I would have to make a bike trip to the lake before I left town. Hopefully, I will have a few more days until my truck is fixed. Coming up to Chris's farm, I glance over and see him at the barn. He looked good in his T-shirt, jeans, and boots. As I looked him over, he must have felt my stare and looked right at me. Crap, what do I do now? Should I stop in, wave, or keep going? Why was this such a big decision? Turning my bike, I pulled in the driveway and headed toward the barn. "Hey!" I said, jumping off the bike. Holding onto the handlebars, I walked the bike over to him. He watched me the whole way, which made me feel self-conscious.

"Heading into town?" he asked.

"Yep. Today I'm turning left at the light and checking out the other side of the road. Hopefully Pete has had a chance to look at my truck and will be able to tell me what the damage is going to be to my wallet."

"He's great at what he does. If it can be fixed, he will fix it. He won't screw you over either. Sometimes, I'm not even sure how he survives charging so little for his work. Do you want me to go with you?"

Thinking it over, I thought this might be the perfect opportunity to get to know Chris better. Quickly changing my mind, I said, "No, that's okay. I want to go to the library and spend some time getting a few books. I also have to go back to the grocery store to get some things I forgot yesterday. So it will probably be an all-day event. If you are around on my way back, I'll stop in and tell you what I found out about the truck."

Nodding, Chris responded, "Sounds good. Tell Pete I said hello."

Jumping on the bike, I gave it a little push off. "Talk with you later. If you aren't around, I'll just give you a call." Lifting his hand, we gave a wave, and I headed back on my way.

Chapter 5

The town came quicker today. Maybe it just seemed that way because I knew where I was going. Taking a left at the light, I rode past the library and headed directly to Pete's. The bell jingled as I walked through the door. Pete was at the counter, writing something up. Looking up, he announced, "You're just in time. Do you want the good news or the bad news first?"

"Give me the good news," I said, holding up crossed fingers.

"Well there isn't really any good news, except you're living next to the best bakery in town. You have to try the blueberry pillows."

Oh crap, I thought as he continued.

"The bad news is that Chris was right. It is the transmission. I just got off the phone with my supplier. It is going to take at least a few weeks to get the parts up here. There has been a backorder on parts for some time now. It isn't going to be cheap either. You're looking at at least $3,000."

"Yikes, that is bad." I didn't want to say that that was all the money I had planned for the summer. It looked like my adventure would be coming to an end before it even got started. I wanted to cry.

"I'll try to do it as inexpensively as I can." He interrupted my thoughts. He could obviously see the panic in my eyes.

"Oh, Chris told me that I can trust you. Give me a call with any updates. Thank you." Leaving the way I came, I decided to just walk the bike back over to the library.

Walking through the front door, I took a deep breath. I loved the smell of old books. It seemed like everyone just read books online any more, but not me. The feel and smell of a book in my hand was part of what I liked about reading. It was part of the whole experience. When I was in college, I dreamed of opening up a used book coffee shop. People could come in to read and just drink coffee all day long. When my dad got sick, I forgot all about that idea. The truth is, I forgot all about it until right now.

Walking up to the counter, a young man stood behind the desk. He was tall and thin with wire-rimmed glasses that made him look the part. Adding to his look was his blue shirt and red bow tie, which seemed like a bit much for the area, but what did I know? "Good morning. Can I help you find a book?"

"Well, I'm just in town for a little while. Would I be able to check any books out?"

"Do you have a license?" he asked. Without answering, I reached into my pocket and pulled out my phone. Snapping off the case, I grabbed my license and handed it to him. "You know, you shouldn't really keep your license in the back of your phone," he lectured. "If you lose your phone, then you lose your license too." He took my license and walked to his computer. When he was done entering my information, he handed it back to me. Unsnapping the case again, I tried to hide the fact that my credit card was behind the phone too. I didn't really feel like being lectured about losing my phone, license, and credit card by a twenty-year-old fashion-savvy librarian. "Looking for anything particular?"

"No, just looking for some quick reads." I sure wasn't going to tell some young guy that I got my kicks off of reading trash novels. Looking around, I hoped they had a self-checkout. I'd rather keep this secret to myself.

After finding two books, I decided that would probably last me until the end of the week. After loading them into the basket, I jumped on the bike and headed back to the grocery store. The first stop was the candy counter. Connie was working again. "Hi, Melissa. What can I get you today?" Looking up and down the counter, I tried to make a decision. More than anything, I wanted to get a pack of the candy cigarettes. I hadn't seen those in years, and I used to love them as a kid. I thought I could give Kathy a great impression of what Connie looked like on her smoke break. I decided that was just mean, and I kept looking.

As I walked up and down the counter, Connie started in. "Did you find out anything about your truck?" Looking out at my bike, she must have eagle eyes because she spotted the books. "Oh I see you went to the library. Did you get a chance to meet Chad?" I nodded, and she continued without taking a breath. "Chad graduated from Michigan State last year with a degree in library science. I didn't even know that was a thing. His mom was the librarian in town for the last twenty years. When Chad was younger, she would bring him to work every day, and he would just read and read. He is better with books than he is with women. That is probably why he is still single. Plus, he likes to dress like he lives in New York City instead of a small town. Bow ties aren't really for every girl, if you know what I mean. Anyway, his mom retired when he came back to town so that he could take over her job. She is afraid he will move far away and she will just be left behind with just her husband."

I wondered how Connie could talk so much without really taking a breath. I guess her lungs were probably used to having no air from smoking so much. "I think I will get some dark chocolate-covered pretzels and some of those red and black raspberry gummies."

I grabbed my bags and headed back to get my margarita mix and coffee filters. I stopped by the cooler to see if there was anything I could grab for dinner. I decided on a pack of hot dogs, buns, some chili, and some shredded cheese. Thinking in my head about Pete, I might have seemed a little short with him. I was just surprised at the cost of the transmission. I hope he didn't think I was a jerk. Heading back to the candy counter, I ordered a chocolate shake to go.

I loaded the basket but kept the shake in my hand. When I headed back to Pete's, the overhead doors were open. Riding my bike in, I could see Pete lying under another car. As he slid out, I said, "Don't get up. I got you a shake from the store. I know before I seemed a little short when you told me the cost. I didn't want you to think I wasn't appreciative. I was just a little shocked. Plus, I forgot to tell you that Chris said hello." Setting down the shake, I jumped back on the bike before he could say anything. "Talk to you later."

Thinking everything over in my head, I was feeling a little overwhelmed. I knew I could call my mom and ask for money, but I didn't want to go that route. Maybe I could talk to Kathy to see if she needed any help for the next few weeks. Before I knew it, I was home. I had forgotten to look to see if Chris was home. Maybe I would just give him a call.

Unloading the basket, this time, I could hear his truck pull in the driveway. "Hey, Mel," he said as he walked toward me. "You rode right past me without stopping in."

Still holding the bags, I decided I liked the way he called me Mel. I think he could call me anything, and I would still like it. "Oh, I'm sorry. I talked to Pete. It's going to be around three grand to fix my truck. I was thinking everything through and forgot all about stopping."

Looking in my basket at the books, Chris smiled when he saw the long-haired man holding onto the woman in the flowing dress on the cover of my romance novel. Grabbing the books quickly, I tried to hide them in my bag. "Want to come in and have some dinner? I make a mean chili dog."

"Sure," he said, following me inside. "Do you want me to hide my truck around the back in case someone drives by?"

Laughing, I said, "I think I'll risk it. Plus, it will make Connie crazy."

Chapter 6

Chris sat down at the old kitchen table, as I started emptying the grocery bag. Grabbing the bags of candy, I chucked them at Chris. "Here's a snack while you're waiting." Setting down the gummies, he untied the bag of chocolate-covered pretzels. A man after my own heart. "So how's the farm?" In my mind, that sounded like a good conversation starter, but when I said it out loud, it sounded stupid. I could feel my face heating up. Turning toward the stove, I put my back to Chris.

Taking a deep breath, he began, "The farm is the farm. I took it over when my parents couldn't do it anymore. I started off by helping my mom after my dad got Alzheimer's disease. One day, he went out to the barn and couldn't remember how to run the tractor. He had been working in that same field for forty years. It was downhill after that. Eventually my mom asked me if I wanted to buy the farm. I have been farming ever since. At one point, I considered going to college, but that isn't how life worked out for me."

We talked and talked. After dinner, I washed, and he dried the dishes. After finishing up, Chris took the dishrag off his shoulder. "I did buy some margarita mix today. Do you want to have a drink on the porch?"

"I better head home now, plus I'm not really a drinker." I felt a little embarrassed. "It was nice to have someone to actually talk with tonight. I never really talked to someone about my parents before. Thanks for listening."

Walking Chris outside, I joked with Chris, "Why don't you leave your truck here tonight and just take the bike home? That way, we can really get everyone in town talking."

Chris laughed out loud, "Yeah, and I will stop in town tomorrow at lunchtime to see how many people are getting a milkshake and the latest gossip."

We just looked at each other smiling, not knowing what the protocol was for goodbye. I couldn't take the pressure and just decided to hug him. He felt good and strong. He felt like I imagined the long-haired, shirtless man looked like on the cover of my book. "After I leave town, you won't be able to eat another chili dog without thinking about me."

"That is probably true," he said and headed toward his truck.

I stood there smiling until he pulled out of the driveway. Walking directly back to the kitchen, I grabbed the largest glass I could find. I opened the freezer and filled the old plastic Miller Lite mug with ice cubes from the tray. Filling the glass to the rim, I took a quick sip, then refilled the glass. With a cup in hand, I headed toward the front porch swing. I grabbed my library book off the counter and immediately set it back down. I think tonight I would just relax and enjoy the country air. Sitting there, I hoped Pete wouldn't rush on getting my truck fixed.

Chapter 7

I'm not sure if it was the bed or the air that made me fall asleep so fast. But the next thing I knew, I was wide awake. I had to go to the bathroom anyway. Looking out the window, the bakery light wasn't on yet. It wasn't even 3 a.m. Instead of seeing a light, I could see three cows standing in the driveway by the light of the moon. Their constant mooing made it impossible to go back to sleep. By morning, I had decided I was having burgers for dinner. I had never wanted a burger more in all my life.

Heading outside in the morning, the cows were gone now. Looking up, I could see seagulls flying overhead. It was windier than it had been since I arrived. The sky was cloudy, and it looked dark. My plan to take the bike to the beach today would have to be put on hold. I didn't want to ride ten miles down the road and the rain to start. I decided today would be a good day for just reading. But first, I needed a doughnut.

The young girl at the counter was back. I recognized the man talking to her as Chad from the library. Hmmm, I thought. I wonder if Kathy had a hand in this matchmaking too. "Hi, Chad." I started, looking at the girl behind the counter. "He helped me get a library card yesterday. He was super helpful."

"Oh he's the best," she continued. "He is also one of my favorite volunteer firemen." Ah, I thought. He had come in on the first day I was in town. He was one of the firemen that had stopped by on their way back from a fire. I'm guessing it was his idea to stop and get a doughnut before dropping off the fire truck at the station. Smooth move, Chad. A woman does love a man in uniform. However, I imagined he probably had a bow tie underneath his yellow fireman jacket.

"I didn't know you knew Abby," he said. "I wouldn't have required your license if I knew you knew Abby. She is a great judge of character." Abby laughed and patted Chad on the hand. Reaching up, she straightened his yellow bow tie. Connie was wrong. Apparently some women really do like bow ties. "Did you get a wallet for your license yet?"

Grabbing my long john, I ignored Chad's question and headed toward the coffee. Propping the door open, I sat at the picnic table and faced inward. I learned my lesson last time. With the door open, I could hear Abby giggling with Chad. Kathy was in the back, baking bread. I watched her until she looked up and then waved. Holding up her finger, she let me know she would be out in a few minutes.

"Hi honey. I saw Chris was at your house last night for dinner. You didn't think you were going to get away with not filling me in on all the juicy gossip, right? I checked on the way in to work this morning to see if his truck was still in your driveway. Unfortunately, all I saw were those damn cows. I spent the morning with the owners trying to get them back into their pen. The wire fence went out last night, and they got out. So I'm guessing you didn't get lucky last night. Did you at least get a kiss?"

"Oh my gosh, Kathy." I laughed. I liked her more every time I talked to her. "No, but I did get a nice hug, and from what I can tell, he hauls a lot of hay."

"If that's code for 'being well endowed,' who knows. I don't think he has been on more than a handful of dates since he broke it off with his high school girlfriend years ago."

"No, I wasn't talking in code." I laughed. "I meant he had strong arms from working on the farm. We didn't even kiss. And I heard all about Cyndee from Connie. That seemed like a terrible situation."

"Yeah, it was, and it wasn't. I think Cyndee wanted to break it off with Chris before she went to school. She never really wanted to go to college anyway. When she graduated from high school, she told her parents she wanted to go to beauty school, and her parents told her she couldn't go to beauty school and live under their roof. So she went to college. They were the ones who really liked Chris too. I personally think she might have gotten pregnant on purpose.

I think that was her way of getting out of college and breaking up with Chris at the same time. After Christmas break, she immediately started beauty school. She was finished by the time she had the baby. Her salon is in the hardware building on the second floor. I think you would probably like her. Chris never realized that she did him a favor. She just wasn't strong enough to stand up to her parents about anything. And crap, not even a kiss? That boy is always so respectable. Maybe you can change that."

We laughed and talked as I finished my doughnut. I decided that I would hate Cyndee whether or not Kathy thought I would like her. It was a matter of principle. I told her about Pete and the bad news about the truck. She sat there and suddenly stood up. "Come with me."

She walked back behind the glass, and I followed her. "See this," she said pointing to a rack full of empty metal doughnut sheets. "See that," she said pointing next to the wooden table at two large mixing bowls. "I'm a baker, not a dishwasher. What do you think of the idea of working here a few hours a day? All you would have to do is wash the metal doughnut trays, mixers, and some bread pans. It won't take you long, and it will really help me out. Plus, then I can keep tabs on you and Chris and make sure neither one of you two screws this up. I can't pay much, but you could stay in the house for free. Handing me a towel and a bucket with bleach, she continued, "You can start now."

Two hours later, I was walking back across the field in the rain. The drops felt great after being in the hot bakery for only a few hours. How I ended up with a job washing dishes in a bakery, I wasn't sure. I tried to replay the conversation with Kathy in my head to see how it all went down. I was too tired to think. At some point this morning, I made the plan to just spend the rest of the day reading books on the swing, and that is what I was going to do.

Grabbing my books, I decided I would just sit down on the couch for a few seconds and rest my eyes before heading out to the swing. I was suddenly awakened when my phone hit the floor. Picking it up, I glanced at the time, 2 p.m. What? I had fallen asleep for three hours. Apparently, I didn't sleep at all the night before because of those stupid cows. Looking outside, it was pouring rain. There was no way to get to the grocery store to buy some burgers. I decided I would just make myself an egg salad sandwich tonight and would try to head into town tomorrow. I checked my phone again, hoping I had missed a call from Chris. Nothing. Disappointed, I headed out to the swing. I could at least get my romance fix through my trashy novels.

A few hours later, I folded the corner of the book and decided to go make myself dinner. Reaching for the drawer, I noticed the knob was loose. I should probably head to the hardware store in the morning and pick up some screws and a screwdriver. Raising my eyebrows up and down and letting out an evil laugh, I announced out loud to myself, "Maybe I'll get my hair trimmed too. Oh my gosh, I think I have lost my mind."

Chapter 8

My phone rang right as I was heading out to start my second day of work. I hoped it was Chris, but it was Pete. He was able to find a rebuilt transmission that could be delivered early next week. Plus, it was going to save me around $1000. Clapping my hands, I almost ran to the bakery to tell Kathy the good news.

"Good morning, Abby!" I said rushing past her and into the kitchen to where Kathy was working. I couldn't wait to give her the good news.

"I knew Pete would take care of you," she said as she hugged me. "But more importantly, has Chris been taking care of you?"

"I haven't seen or heard from him since we had dinner the other night. Maybe it didn't go as well as I thought. I have to go into town this afternoon. Maybe I'll see if he's around."

Nodding her head, she walked back to her mixer and continued mixing the bread dough. "Maybe I'll have to stick a knife in the plug and see if Chris can come fix it." As I filled the sink with water, I could hear her yell at me, "I'll do it too." Laughing, I didn't respond.

Time flew by that morning. I was just finishing up when the school bus pulled into the parking lot. Oh yeah, I forgot the elementary school kids were coming for a tour of the bakery. "The school thinks I am dedicating my time to future leaders of our community," Kathy laughed. "But really I'm using my doughnuts as a kind of gateway drug. Once they have a taste of my doughnuts, they will never be able to quit coming to this bakery. Doughnuts today, pies tomorrow, future sugar addicts of America." As Kathy grabbed the doughnut trays, I could hear the kids scream with excitement as she let them each grab one. While racing out the door, I waved a quick goodbye without even stopping.

The nice cold shower felt good this morning. I decided against wearing a baseball hat. After brushing my hair out, I thought I would leave it down and let it dry in the wind. Putting on sunscreen, I decided I would wear a little mascara and eyeliner today. That was pretty much my max routine for makeup. Occasionally I would wear lipstick, but usually only at Christmas and Easter. I reached into my makeup bag and pulled out a stick of vanilla Burt's Bees Lip Balm. What good is it to have sunscreen on your face if you have wrinkled old witch lips? Pressing my lips together, I looked in the mirror. Good enough, I decided.

The first stop was the library. Walking in, Chad had his back to the door. I slipped the books in the return slot before he saw me and headed toward the center rack labeled, "New Releases." I decided that I would only grab one book today. When Chad went in the back to grab a phone call, I raced to the self-checkout so he wouldn't see me grabbing the library card from behind my phone case. As he hung up the phone, I gave a quick wave and headed toward the door. "Have a good day," I could hear as the door shut behind me. Mission accomplished.

Walking my bike through the light, I looked up toward the second floor of the hardware shop while I was still in the middle of the street. I could see Cyndee's salon sign "Curl Up and Dye" was lit up. I was too far away, and the windows were tinted, so I couldn't see anyone. Wedging my bike between the large pile of bags of mulch and the red brick wall, I headed inside.

As I entered, a big white pit bull with black spots and black hind legs headed toward me. I debated leaving, but an old woman from behind the counter yelled to me, "He won't hurt you. He's a lover, not a fighter." I recognized her as the old woman that was drinking a shake at the grocery store gossiping with Connie on my first trip into town.

As I bent down and grabbed his face, I petted behind both his ears. "Hey buddy, what's your name?"

"That's Ruger. He's our guard dog, but I think if anyone ever tried to rob us, he would just lick them to death." I imagined she said that at least once a day. "Looking for anything?"

"Just looking around." I smiled. It was more like just nosing around, glancing to see if there was a visible stairway that headed up to the salon.

"Well, grab some popcorn. We have anything you could ever want."

Walking toward the counter, a large glass popcorn machine sat on a red cart that had wheels. The smell was intoxicating. I grabbed a brown lunch bag and opened the glass. Grabbing out the metal scoop, I filled my bag to the brim. Shutting the door, I walked to the large display of bird feeders.

I had to admit, I had never seen a hardware store like this before. The walls were lined with cabinets that displayed hundreds of knobs and handles, from antique to modern. Metal house numbers in different fonts were hanging in different colors and sizes on an entire wall. A glass cabinet near the back was filled with handguns, knives, ammunition, and fishing reels. Behind the counter were lines of fishing poles, shotguns, and rifles.

Over an hour later, I was at the front counter with an empty popcorn bag, a glass hummingbird feeder, a jar of red sugar water, and a Phillips screwdriver. "I could spend the entire day here." The woman looked at me, quite proud of herself.

"This store has been in my family for over sixty years. We remodeled about six years back and added a small apartment and a beauty salon on the second floor." Looking at her, I hoped that she would ask if I wanted to take a look upstairs, but she didn't. Handing me my change, she said, "We have popcorn every day. Feel free to just stop in for a bag."

Before heading into the house, I filled the bird feeder up with bird food. Looking around, I tried to find a good place to hang it. On the corner of the porch rail, I spotted a small cast iron hook where I imagined a plant once hung. Reaching up on my tip toes, I attached the chain from the top of the bird feeder to the hook. Walking back to the swing, I sat down for a second and looked at the feeder. Perfect, I thought. Reaching into my pocket, I grabbed out my lip balm. Rubbing it on my lips, I felt a sense of accomplishment. Standing back up, I headed inside.

As my soup heated on the stove, I grabbed the screwdriver from the bag and opened the broken drawer. Tightening the screw attached to the nob took only a few seconds. Thinking it over, I realized I spent over an hour in a hardware store buying a screwdriver to make a thirty-second fix. The truth is, I made that trip to see if Cyndee was the woman I imagined her to be. I didn't even do that. At least, the hardware store was incredible, and the popcorn was good.

The vibration of my phone startled me out of my thoughts. Picking it up, Kathy was on the other line. "Hi honey," she started. "Any chance you can come in early in the morning tomorrow? I am afraid I won't be able to have everything done in time for the school event. I need all the help I can get."

"Of course, what time do you need me?" I should have asked the question before I agreed.

"Okay, see you at five." I hung up the phone and set the alarm on my phone. I'd have to get up by 4:15. I decided to go to bed early again, right after *Jeopardy*.

Chapter 9

The next morning came very early. Walking over to the bakery in the dark was a little scary. I decided that I would walk down the street instead of cutting through the field. I didn't want to trip, and honestly, I was kind of afraid I would be attacked by some raccoons or possums or anything else that us, city folk, think comes out after dark. When I arrived, Abby was already there. She was back in the kitchen with Kathy, helping powder and sugar the hot doughnuts.

"Come on back," Kathy said, pointing to a large pile of boxes. "We need to start packing up the doughnuts. The ones on the rack are ready to go." Kathy was focused as she shouted out her instructions.

Grabbing the first tray, I asked, "What's going on at the school?"

Abby jumped in, her eyes smiling, "Only the best day for every senior class. It's Drive Your Tractor to School Day. Every senior gets to drive their family's farm tractor to school. Starting around 6:30, everyone starts leaving their house on their tractor. As you get closer and closer to the school, it's like a huge parade of tractors with every senior joining in. If you don't have a tractor, you can ride a quad or a dirt bike or just ride with a friend. When the first tractor gets to school, they head down to the football field where all the lower class-men are sitting in stands. Each tractor takes a turn around the track and then heads up to the parking lot. When every tractor has gone around the track, the entire school walks around the parking lot and looks at all the different tractors."

Kathy interrupted, "And they all want to be eating our hot doughnuts. The school orders them every year. It's part of the event. So we have to get these packed and loaded on the wagon. Chris will be here soon with his tractor and wagon. We can't show up to Take Your Tractor to School Day in my old truck. He helps every year. We need to be at school before the first kid leaves his farm, so let's get moving."

I didn't have much time to think about the fact that I wished I would have at least washed my face before heading out the door. If I knew Chris was coming, I would have tried harder. When Chris arrived, he smiled when he saw me. "Ah, looks like we have some extra help this year." Grabbing the boxes, he started taking load after load of the boxes to the wagon until it was completely filled.

"Abby and I will ride on the wagon to make sure the doughnuts are safe." Looking at me, she continued, "Have you ever ridden on a tractor before?" I didn't have time to answer when she looked at Chris. "She can ride you, I mean with you." Chris shot a look at her, but Kathy ignored him.

"This isn't the tractor you were in the other day, was it?" I asked Chis as he helped me onto the flat wooden bench."

"No," he laughed, as if I should have known. "We just use this one for parades or antique tractor shows. Occasionally an old friend of my dad's might stop by to see it. Oh, and every year, the school asks to use it for a float for the homecoming game."

Riding down the road was slow, loud, and amazing. I would never have imagined that you sat up so high in a tractor, but the tires were huge. Chris would occasionally look over at me and smile. He laughed when I said, "This is the greatest thing I have ever done in my entire life." I also thought it was incredibly romantic. I only wished I was sitting closer to Chris.

When I looked back at Abby and Kathy to make sure they were doing all right, they were talking to each other. I couldn't hear what they were saying, but Kathy just looked at me and leaned her head to the side and nodded. She tried giving me hints to scoot closer to Chris, but I was as close as I could get. Abby was raising her eyebrows up and down. Then I knew exactly what they were talking about. They were scheming.

The romance quickly ended as we pulled into the parking lot. Chris parked the tractor sideways between the school and the parking lot. Abby and Kathy jumped down and started unloading a large popup tent. Under the tent, they set up a huge table. Chris and I handed the boxes of doughnuts down, and they opened up the boxes and displayed the different types of doughnuts. As the kids walked past our tractor and down to the football field, you could feel their excitement. Chris grabbed my hand and said, "Come on, you have to experience this from the stadium."

He held on to my hand for just a few seconds to guide me where to go and then let go. I wanted to reach over and grab it back. "We'll be back before the kids come for their doughnuts." He assured Kathy, and we headed to the football field.

Standing by the entrance of the track, we watched as the kids drove their tractors onto the track. The crowd roared as each new tractor entered the track. It was super exciting. I was surprised that the tractors were green, red, orange, and blue. Chris would tell me what kind they were as they rode past. Some had large American flags sticking out the back; others had banners with the name of their family farms on them. As they went around the field, some were heading in, and others were leaving, forming kind of a figure eight. When the leading tractors headed up to the parking lot, Chris announced, "We'd better head up to help Kathy. She's going to be attacked by savages pretty soon." Standing as close to him as I could, I tried to touch the back of my hand to his, giving him the hint to grab my hand. He didn't. *He is out of practice*, I thought to myself as we raced up to the doughnut tractor.

When we reached the top of the hill, Abby and Kathy already had their plastic gloves on. Handing me the box, she announced, "Put these on. Chris, you need to make sure the kids stay in line, one doughnut each." She looked at me with concern. "I'm afraid that we might not have enough doughnuts."

An hour later, all the doughnuts were gone, and the kids were heading into school, as slowly as they could. Eventually, a voice came over the speakers announcing that everyone should return to their home room. "Time to head back," Kathy announced. I jumped on the trailer with Abby and let Kathy sit and chat with Chris on the way back to the bakery. It was nice to get to know Abby a little bit better too. She talked about her dream of becoming a veterinarian in town, and she told me all about Chad.

Back at the bakery, Chris helped Kathy down. Abby and I jumped off the trailer. "Mel," Chris called out as Abby and I started into the bakery. Turning around, Kathy walked past without making eye contact with me. "I was talking to Kathy, and she thought maybe we could all head to The Brown Trout tonight to get some of their all-you-can-eat fish fry. Everyone in town usually spends Fridays there."

"Sounds fun." It would be nice if he wanted to do something without any pressure from Kathy.

Entering the bakery, Kathy looked at me and Abby. "You guys can take the rest of the day off. Thanks for all your help this morning."

Abby gave her a quick hug and thank-you and headed out the door. "Want to grab a coffee with me?" Kathy asked.

We both grabbed a doughnut and a cup of coffee and went out to sit at the picnic table. "I feel like you pressured Chris into taking me to the bar tonight," I said as we sat down.

"I didn't pressure him. He spent the whole ride back trying to get information about you. He is just out of practice. I just suggested that we all go to the fish fry tonight. He was only using me as an excuse. May I suggest you jazz yourself up a little tonight? I mean, the baseball hat is cute, but not really on a date."

We talked for at least another hour or two. I found out all about Kathy, her husband, and Chris's family. Apparently he had a sister that was married. Her husband was an alcoholic and abusive. Chris had put a real beating on him one time when he found out he had hit his sister. After that, they moved out of state. Occasionally, she would come visit, but he wouldn't let her come alone. He was afraid Chris would talk her into leaving him. They used to be very close, but now they hardly see each other. It made Chris very sad.

Chapter 10

At around six o'clock, Chris's truck pulled into the driveway. I debated if I should run out to meet him or wait to see if he came up to the door. Looking out the window, I could see him walking up the steps. He was dressed in blue jeans and boots and a button-up short-sleeve gray shirt. I looked down at my own outfit, white T-shirt, jeans, and Converse shoes. Kathy was going to be disappointed. I did put on some lip gloss though. Good enough, I decided as I took one last look in the mirror. I waited until he knocked before going down the stairs.

Opening the door, I felt a little nervous, which I thought was stupid. This wasn't really a date. Everyone was going to be there, Kathy, Abby, Chad, Chris, and me. I wondered if Connie and her boyfriend were going to be there and maybe the nice lady from the hardware store. Maybe Cyndee was going to be there. I had no reason to be nervous. This is just what everyone in town does on Friday nights.

"Hey, Chris, you look nice," I said as I shut the door behind me. "You smell nice too." I stepped closer and leaned into him. He tilted his head as if my breath tickled his neck.

"Yeah, I take a shower every couple of weeks whether I need to or not." He gave me his usual half-smile as he opened my door.

In his truck, I leaned against my door and looked over at him. "I hope Kathy didn't pressure you into bringing me with you tonight." I was a little nervous at what his answer might be, but I figured I was still close enough to home that he could bring me back if he wanted.

"Oh, she did. She twisted my arm until I agreed." Reaching over, he put his hand on my knee and squeezed. "It's actually really nice to have someone to take out besides Kathy. I think she is getting kind of sick of being my date every weekend." I waited for him to take his hand off my knee, but he didn't. Reaching down, I placed my hand on top of his.

As we walked into The Brown Trout, a tall table lined the entire side wall, with bar stools facing toward the bar. On the opposite wall, the bar ran its entire length. A mirror lined the back of the bar so that everyone could see the people that were sitting behind them and the door. When we walked in, everyone yelled, "Hello," to Chris. Taking my hand, Chris led me down a pathway to a few steps that led to a second room. I felt proud, as if he was letting everyone know that we were together.

The second room was filled with more large tables with bench seats. As people entered the bar, they would just sit at whatever table had room available. Seeing Kathy, Abby, and Chad, Chris beelined for the opening.

Sitting down, a waitress dropped off large icy mugs and a fresh pitcher of beer in front of us. "I'll be right back with your fish and chips."

I looked at Kathy inquisitively. "Did you order for us?"

Chris jumped in, "You don't really order here. It's Friday. Friday is beer and fish night. You come in. You get beer and fish. They keep it simple." A few seconds later, the waitress was back with two red plastic baskets overflowing with fried fish and French fries.

"Wave me down when you need your next basket or another pitcher." She raced away and headed to the bar for more pitchers to deliver to other tables. Every time we heard names being yelled out, we knew more people had come in. The entire night, she ran from table to table with baskets and pitchers. The room was filled with friends that have known each other for years. There were old people and young couples with babies, all sharing tables. Everyone was talking loudly and laughing. I watched as Chris and Kathy talked to new people as they joined our table. Abby and Chad moved from our table to another when other younger people came in. I just watched, listened, and smiled the entire night. Occasionally, Chris would reach under the table and squeeze my knee. I liked it when his hand would move up my leg. Kathy would watch and wiggle her eyebrows at me.

As the night grew late, the waitress had stopped bringing fish and was a lot slower at delivering pitchers. Finally, Kathy stood up and said, "I'm gonna call it a night."

"We should probably get going too," Chris said as we all stood up. Waving to Chad and Abby, we headed toward the door. After hugging goodbye to Kathy, Chris and I headed to his truck. The ride back seemed very quiet, mostly because the bar was so loud.

"I can see why everyone goes there on Fridays. I don't think I have ever been to a bar where everyone seems like part of your family."

"It's like that around here. Sometimes it's great. Sometimes it's not. Everyone knows everything about everyone else, or at least, they think they do. Sometimes it makes it hard to move on when everyone keeps talking about what used to be."

I nodded. "Like Cyndee?"

"Exactly. I'm sure you heard about how heartbroken I was, and people think I still am. Truth is, I was hurt. It messed me up for a long time, especially seeing her and her baby every time I went into town. I could hear people whispering, and so could she. But as time went on, I felt less pissed and more sympathetic toward her. She has been a single mom for over six years now. She is a great mom that works really hard. She doesn't go to The Brown Trout because she is tired from working so much and just wants time to spend with her little girl. We were just young. We made mistakes. We just weren't meant to be. People still talk, but it doesn't bother me anymore. They think I don't date because I haven't gotten over her, but I have been just trying to take care of the farm. After I lost my parents, I had to take care of all their affairs. I had to learn things that I was too dumb to learn when my dad tried to teach me. I have a sister that I don't see and I worry about. It's a long story, but her husband is an idiot. If I call her, she won't answer the phone if he is around. If we talk, she will have to hang up if he comes home. I have been trying to get her to move back, but she isn't ready to leave him yet. I am afraid something will happen, and she won't be able to leave. Anyway, I am over Cyndee. She was over me before I was over her, but we both want good things for each other." Pulling into the driveway, he finished,

"This is the first time in a while that I have really enjoyed myself. I can't remember just laughing like I did tonight in a very long time."

"Same." I answered, smiling and raising my shoulders in contentment. "Thanks for everything. I feel like I have been thanking you ever since we first met." He smiled and walked with me to the doorway. "Good night."

Reaching up, Chris grabbed my face and gently kissed my lips. "Good night,'" he said. I watched him walk back to his truck. When the light came on, I waved and went into the house.

It was late, and I was tired. I wanted to call my mom and tell her everything. Instead, I went into the kitchen and made myself a margarita. Then I headed upstairs, and I started the bathwater. I poured some shampoo in the water, trying to make a nice bubble bath. As I lay in the water and sipped my drink, I thought about the evening. Chewing my ice, I realized I was both excited and nervous about what the future might hold.

Chapter 11

I hadn't even dried off when my phone began to vibrate. Looking down at it, I could see it was Kathy. Oh my gosh, I laughed with excitement. She can't even wait until morning to hear all about Chris and me. I thought I would let it buzz a little while longer, just to punish her. Truthfully, I was so glad she was calling. I wanted to tell her every detail. Finally, I picked it up and laughed, "No, Chris isn't spending the night."

"Melissa, it's Chad. Kathy has had a heart attack." I couldn't comprehend what I heard.

"What?" I said with panic. "What happened?"

"The ambulance just took Kathy to the hospital. I already called Chris. He is on his way to pick you up."

Hanging up, I quickly threw on a pair of sweatpants and a T-shirt and raced downstairs. I had barely made it to the door when I saw dirt flying everywhere in the driveway. Chris was driving unbelievably fast toward the house. I ran out the door and jumped into his truck before he even had a chance to slow down. Looking over at Chris, he didn't say anything to me. His jaw was locked tightly together, and his eyes steered straight ahead. The crease between his eyes seemed extra deep.

There wasn't a hospital in town, so we had to drive thirty minutes. "She's going to be okay," I whispered, but Chris just stayed focused on the road. Kathy was already in surgery, when we arrived at the hospital. We sat in the waiting area and waited to hear from the doctor on her status. Hours went by before the doctor came back. Chris ran to meet him by the door. They stepped into the hallway, and I wasn't able to hear what they were saying. When he came back in, Chad and Abby were with him.

"She made it through surgery okay. We won't be able to see her until tomorrow." Chris hugged me with relief. "She isn't out of the woods yet, but the doctor thinks she will be okay." We decided to head home to get a few hours of sleep.

Standing in the parking lot, Abby said she was going to head to the bakery early. The bakery was Kathy's livelihood. "We need Kathy to get better. If she wakes up tomorrow and her bakery is closed, she will never focus on getting better." She promised to make a few phone calls and would meet me in the morning.

When we pulled into the driveway, I looked at Chris. He could barely keep his eyes open. "Would you like to stay here tonight with me? I won't be much comfort, but at least, you won't have to be alone."

He smiled and pulled me in for a hug. "It sounds like you are going to have a very early morning. I think I will let you get some rest. I will head to the hospital in the morning and will stop in the bakery and give you an update."

"Okay, good night." He kissed my forehead and headed home. I didn't even take off my sweatpants and T-shirt before falling into bed. The last thing I remember was setting my alarm for 2:45.

Chapter 12

It seemed like I had barely shut my eyes when my alarm went off. Jumping up, I didn't give myself time to think. By 3 a.m., I was almost at the bakery. It was weird seeing the bakery so dark. I was just going inside when I heard some cars pull up. It was Abby and an older woman. Hugging me, Abby started, "This is my mom, Patty. She grew up with Kathy. She worked here when I was little. She is going to help make the bread." Before Patty started cooking the bread, she showed Abby and me how to make the doughnuts. Then she taught us how to work the fryer. It was tricky at first. We had to take the huge bowl of dough and pour it into this bowl that was on an arm above the fryer. Starting at the far end, I would drag the bowl across the oil, pulling the trigger button. With every pull, a little circle of dough would drop out into the oil. The goal would be to drop three doughnuts next to each other, before you started the next row.

It took about ten rows for my doughnuts to actually look like circles and not hot dog buns. We threw the first batch of deformed doughnuts underneath the counter into a five-gallon bucket. Patty said she would take the ugly doughnuts home for her pigs. Who knew that pigs ate doughnuts?

The shape of the doughnuts looked better as the morning went on. As the doughnuts fried, Abby would grab them off the rack and put them on a tray. The first trays, she powdered and cinnamon sugared while they were still hot. Patty explained that we had to do it while they were hot so the sugar would stick. As I filled the rack with doughnuts, Abby would wait for them to cool and frost them. When Abby was done frosting, she headed upfront to work the counter.

As Patty continued working on the bread, she called me over. She opened the drawer underneath the wooden table and showed me the calendar. Each day was marked with which bread to make. The drawer was also filled with piles of laminated recipes. She showed me how to work the mixers and the oven. "Don't worry," she said. "I'll be here tomorrow too."

It was 11 a.m. before I even got a chance to grab some coffee. As I was heading toward the table, Chris walked in front of me. His eyes looked as tired as I felt. "How are you holding up?" he started.

"I'm fine. How's Kathy?" I said, sitting down for the first time all morning.

"She isn't awake yet. I thought maybe we could head over there when you're done. I just talked to Abby, and Chad's mom is going to come over and help with the counter. That should give you a little bit of a rest this afternoon.

"Is this what people in a small town do? Just show up when someone needs you." When my dad was sick, no one helped my mom out besides me, I thought to myself.

"It's what we do. Now you sit there for a few minutes and take a break. I'll finish up with the dishes."

I only sat for a few minutes and then headed back to help Chris with the dishes. Chad's mom came in with the front counter while Abby mopped the floor. Before long, I was ready to leave. *Thank God, tomorrow is Sunday*, I thought. *The bakery is closed, and I can sleep in.*

Chapter 13

Chris and I headed directly to the hospital. Kathy was sitting up in her bed eating dinner when we walked into her room. "I'm the sick one, but you two look terrible."

"How are you feeling?" I asked.

"Not bad, really. Apparently God doesn't want to take me yet." Kathy went on and explained that the doctor had put in two stents and a pacemaker for good luck. "They are going to send me home tomorrow already. I don't know what I am going to do for the next few weeks about the bakery. He said I couldn't work."

"Oh Mel and Abby already worked it all out. They got there first thing this morning," Chris explained.

"Really, Abby figured it all out. She called her mom, and they met me at the bakery at 3 a.m. Patty made the bread and showed us how to make the doughnuts. Chad's mom helped us this afternoon. It took five of us, counting Chris, to do what you usually do. No wonder you had a heart attack." I reached over and held her hand. "So you have nothing to worry about. You just need to get better."

Kathy's eyes were filled with tears. "We better let you get some rest now." Chris stood up. Grabbing my arm, Chris led me toward the door. "I'll be here tomorrow to take you home."

Chris dropped me off at home. We both decided to skip dinner. I just wanted to sleep, and Chris had more work to do at the farm. I jumped in the shower to rinse off the smell of the bakery. Sitting down on the couch, I picked up my phone to call my mom. One missed call. Checking my messages, it was Pete. He would have my truck done by the end of the week. I would be glad to finally be able to drive again. The first stop was the beach.

Chapter 14

The next couple of weeks were exhausting. The usual crew came in to help out while Kathy was recovering. We were all ready for Kathy to come back. The bakery was extremely packed on her first day back. The elementary school kids had all made cards for her and dropped them off at the bakery. The high school's honor society had made a Welcome Back banner to hang on the front door. It was so nice for Kathy to see how much everyone loved her.

"So fill me in on everything," Kathy said when we finally sat down for a break. "How are you and Chris?"

"We are good. He was really scared when he thought he might lose you. To be honest, though, we have both been super busy and haven't been able to spend a lot of time together outside of work. Did you see how Pete fixed my truck? I picked it up at the end of last week. It has been running great. I am debating what I should do now though. I never really planned to just stay here all summer, only until my truck was fixed. But now, I feel like you are my second mom. And Chris, I am not sure what will even happen there."

"Well you can stay in the farmhouse as long as you need to. It was just sitting there empty. It is nice to see some life in it again. Plus, you have helped me out so much with the bakery. I'm not sure what I would do if you left now. I might just have another heart attack. But no pressure to stay. Chris doesn't say much, but I haven't seen him this happy for a while. Now get out of here," she said, standing up. "It feels good working, so I better keep at it before I change my mind."

Hugging her, I whispered, "I'm glad you're back." Walking back to the farm, it was already getting very hot. Today was the perfect day to drive to the beach. I made a plan to go into town and get some candy and a new book. I went over in my head what I needed to grab: a towel, sunglasses, a cooler, Vernors, and my headphones. I rushed the rest of the way home with excitement.

After I loaded the truck, I headed downtown. The first stop was the library. Chad was working the front desk as usual. When I checked out at the front desk, I grabbed my library card out of my new wallet. "Picked this baby up at the gas station," I announced, flashing the wallet in front of him. "Someone suggested I buy one, but I can't remember who it was though."

"Must have been someone very smart." He reached up and straightened his tie with pride.

"I doubt it. See you later." I waved.

Jumping into my truck, I headed toward the grocery store. Getting out, I recognized some of the people on the sidewalk, even though I didn't know their names. They waved at me and asked how Kathy was doing. I tried not to be short, but I wanted to spend as much time on the beach today as possible. There was no time for small talk.

Walking into the store, Connie announced, "Well there she is. Not working today?"

"I'm already done. Kathy is back now."

"Oh I heard." *Of course, you have*, I thought. "So do you have big plans for today?"

"Just heading down to the beach. You know I need to get my candy first."

She laughed. "Chris going with you? I heard you two are quite a pair now. I would have never guessed that one." She wasn't really trying to insult me, just stating a fact. "What can I get you?" I decided on more fireball jawbreakers and Milk Duds. Heading up to the counter, I grabbed two bottles of Vernors. I only really needed one, but I knew if I bought two, Connie would wonder if Chris was coming. I never did answer her question. Jumping in the truck, I spotted Connie looking out the front window. I knew it was killing her not knowing.

I smiled all the way to the beach. The windows were down, and my music was playing. When my mind started to wonder and think about leaving, I just turned the music up loud enough to block out my thoughts. Today was just going to be a day of sun and relaxation.

There were only a few other cars at that beach when I got there. I was able to park right next to the sand. I popped the lid of the cooler and put my candy and Vernors inside. I wrapped my book in the towel and put it on top of the lid. Reaching up, I grabbed my sunglasses from the visor. Kicking my sandals, I decided to leave them on the floor of the truck. Jumping down barefooted, I grabbed the cooler and headed to find the perfect spot.

Looking around, I could see some college kids flying kites. They were running up and down the sand trying to keep the kites in the air. The last thing I wanted was to have sand thrown at me while I was trying to relax. On the other side of the beach, a younger woman with her daughter sat near the water. They were using a plastic pail to dig holes and make sand castles. I picked a spot far enough away that they wouldn't try to make small talk with me. Grabbing my towel, I laid it down. Taking my shirt and shorts off, I wrapped them in a ball to use as a pillow.

I set the book near the cooler and decided to just relax a little bit before starting my book. Tucking my clothes under my head, I realized I forgot to pack sunscreen. Checking the time on my phone, I decided to flip over in twenty minutes so I wouldn't burn.

Lying there, I tried to shut my eyes for a quick nap. In the distance, I could hear the mother and daughter laughing. It made me smile. Pulling my bikini bottoms down a little near my belly, I checked my tan line. Before flipping over, I thought I would take a quick jump in the water to cool off.

Walking toward the beach, the sand was hot. It felt nice when I got to the water. Walking in slowly, I lifted my hands so that my arms weren't touching the water. Deeper and deeper, I walked until I decided to just jump in. Popping out, I raced back to shore. The mom and girl laughed at me as I ran to my towel. I went from burning hot to freezing cold. Flopping on my belly, I decided to let the sun dry me off.

When I felt refreshed, I sat up on my towel. Reaching into the cooler, I opened a Vernors and grabbed my Milk Duds. I watched as the mom and child walked back and forth in front of the water look-ing for rocks. Every time the girl would find one, she would show her mom, who would take it and put it in the bucket. I watched as the little girl pointed to me. Oh no, I thought. They're coming over. I tried to look away, but it was too late.

The girl came up cautiously, followed closely by her mom. "Want to see the rocks that I found?"

"Sure," I said, smiling at her mom.

Her mom mouthed, "Sorry," as the girl sat down.

"My name is Lilly." One by one, she pulled out all the rocks, describing them and setting them on my towel. Her mom sat down in the sand next to me. "Would you like a Vernors?" I asked. "I brought an extra one that I'm not going to drink."

"That would be great," she said. "Want a sip, Lilly?" Lilly took a sip and went right back into describing her rocks. When she was all done, she put them all back in the bucket. Looking at my book, the woman said, "Oh that's a great book. I just finished reading it."

"Oh, I just picked it up today. I love an easy read with a little romance." For some reason, I wasn't embarrassed about telling her. I think it was because she seemed so easy to talk to.

"Same," she said. "I'm Cyndee, by the way. I own the hair salon above the hardware store."

Oh no, it was Cyndee—my archnemesis. I had vowed to hate her before I even met her, and now we were sitting together on the beach sharing a Vernors. *Is it too late to throw her kid off my towel?* I debated. It was too late. I had already started to like her. "I'm Melissa."

"Oh yeah, Connie told me all about you." She laughed. "I'm sure you know all about me too."

I nodded. "Yeah, probably none of it is true about either one of us. Wait until she hears we like each other. Tomorrow is going to be an exciting day at the soda counter." We talked for a while longer until Lilly became bored.

"We better get going, Lilly needs a nap, and it looks like you are getting too much sun." As she headed to pick up her pail, I folded my towel and put my shorts and top over my swimsuit. As I headed toward the truck, I yelled, "Bye, Lilly." They waved, and I drove away.

Chapter 15

Pulling in, I was surprised to see Chris's truck in the drive. Parking next to him, I jumped out of the truck. Chris was on the front swing, just rocking back and forth. Stepping on to the porch, I asked, "How long have you been here?"

"Not long. I like the bird feeder. You had a few hummingbirds." Looking me over, he asked the obvious, "Did you go to the beach?"

I set the cooler by the door and sat next to him. "I love sitting out here and watching the hummingbirds. I got the bird feeder from the hardware store." I was feeling a little guilty that I had spent the afternoon with Cyndee and Lilly. I worried that he might feel I betrayed him. "Yeah, the beach was great. There wasn't hardly anyone there. I did meet Cyndee and Lilly though. They were on the beach playing."

"How was the water?" He ignored what I said about Cyndee.

"It was freezing. I just jumped in and got out right away. I had no idea it would be freezing cold. I hope you don't mind that I talked to Cyndee. I didn't go out of my way to meet her. Lilly ran up to show me the rocks she found, and Cyndee and I started talking. She is nice. I can see why you would have liked her." I felt as though I had to justify why we had talked.

"Yep. That was a long time ago." Chris kept staring at the bird feeder. His tone changed. "Kathy said you are thinking about leaving. Were you even planning on telling me or just sneaking out one night?"

"Really? You think I would just sneak out and not say goodbye. I told Kathy that my plan was never to stay here all summer, and I wasn't sure what I was going to do now that my truck is fixed. I think that is super rude that you even said that." He just ruined my mood.

"Well I think it's rude that you can talk to Kathy about leaving but not talk to me." His eyes narrowed.

"I didn't talk to Kathy about leaving. I said I wasn't sure what I was doing. I also said I wasn't sure what we, you and I, even are. And you know what, just because you got screwed over by Cyndee doesn't mean every other woman you date is going to screw you over. Seriously, it's been over six years. Date me or don't date me, I don't care. But don't act like I am going to just hurt you. I know I didn't grow up here and you haven't known me your entire life, but that doesn't mean I would ever hurt you like that. I never said I was leaving." Standing up, I walked to the door and picked up the cooler. I'm going to wash the sand off now." Going inside, I shut the door behind me.

Chris just looked at me the whole time and didn't say a word. Heading straight back to the kitchen, I jumped up on the counter and stuck my feet in the sink. I hate dirty feet. Starting with the water, I began rinsing the sand out from between my toes. *He has some nerve*, I thought. Yeah, I'm going to pack up my bag in the middle of the night and just leave. What an idiot. Just then, I heard the door open. Before I knew it, Chris was standing next to the counter, "You're an idiot, you know that?" I said, looking at him.

"Yeah, I know." Reaching, he grabbed my waist and turned me around so I was facing him. Standing in between my legs, he pulled me closer and kissed me.

"I'm not planning on leaving. I just told Kathy I wasn't sure what I was doing. What is this?" I asked, pointing to him and then back to me. "If this is just a summer fling, then I need to know that."

"I'm not sure what this is. All I know is you make me happy, happier than I've been in a long time. When Kathy told me that you might be leaving, it pissed me off. I didn't really think you would sneak away in the middle of the night. I just didn't know how to handle it."

"Well you need to get something straight. You make me happy too. When it's time to leave, you will be the first to know." Taking my legs, I wrapped them around his back and squeezed him tighter to me, my arms around his shoulders. I could feel the heat of his body.

"Maybe you can give me a reason to stay." Kissing him, a nice long kiss, my belly filled with butterflies. I had never been kissed like that before. Looking him in the eyes, I smiled, "That might have done it."

Chris stayed a while longer. We talked, and kissed, and kissed some more. I wanted to do more than kiss, but we didn't. We made a plan to hit the concert in the park later that night.

Chapter 16

After changing out of my swimsuit, I took a shower and pulled my hair into a messy bun. Grabbing my red bandanna, I tied it on top of my head and put in my hoop earrings. This is what I looked like the day I met Chris. After throwing on some jean shorts and a T-shirt, I decided to head into town to pick up some fried chicken to eat in the park at the concert.

As I drove to the store, I could feel my face heating up. I wondered if it was from being sunburned or from thinking about the way Chris kissed me. Walking back to the counter, I decided today was the perfect day for a chocolate shake. Connie walked over to greet me. "Need some candy?"

"I sure do. I am going to the concert in the park tonight." I ordered some gummy bears and hot tamales. "Can I get a chocolate malt too? I think I'll just sit down for a while. It's been a busy day."

Connie was delighted that I would keep her company for a while. I knew she would try to weasel out some good gossip. She actually was likable, but I didn't know if I could trust her. She had the gift for gab, and before I knew it, I was telling her about my day at the beach and meeting Cyndee. She was very disappointed that the story didn't end up in a nasty fist fight, but I knew it might be retold in a different way. To her shock, I told her that I could eventually see Cyndee and me as good friends. I finished up when another couple came in to order shakes. "I have to get some more food for the park tonight."

I watched as Connie leaned in and started whispering as I walked away. She couldn't help herself, I decided. I knew better than to give her any information that I didn't want everyone to know. I picked up some chicken and coleslaw from the deli counter. I was glad they had prewrapped plastic silverware that I could just grab too. Heading over to the cooler, I grabbed a four-pack of wine coolers. Sitting in the truck, I texted Chris and asked him to bring a blanket to sit on.

Chris arrived at around six. I was sitting on the front porch swing drinking a margarita when he arrived. Standing up, I ran to the kitchen to grab the food. I was feeling a little light-headed. I realized the only thing I had eaten all day was some Milk Duds and a chocolate malt. Chris waited in the truck until I came out. Jumping in his truck, I realized I liked the way Chris smelled. Leaning over, he kissed me. "Ready?" he asked.

When we arrived at the park, Chris grabbed the blanket from the back seat. I grabbed the food. Then we walked to the park, holding hands. The park had a pavilion that sat at the bottom of the hill. The hill was filled with families on blankets, couples in folding chairs, and single people with their dogs. People were talking and laughing with each other. Chad and Abby were there with both of their parents. Cyndee was there with Lilly. They were eating ice cream sandwiches. When she saw Chris and me, she waved. Chris looked at me and smiled. We both waved back. I thought to myself, maybe it was time that everyone in town moved on. After our little fight, I felt like maybe Chris finally had.

The band played bluegrass for about an hour and a half. I never really listened to bluegrass music before, but it was really enjoyable. Everyone clapped and danced. Chris and I ate the food and watched the crowd. I realized I had three of the four wine coolers. "Of course, you brought candy." He laughed, grabbing the bag of hot tamales.

Standing up to leave, I looked at Chris. "I think I had one too many wine coolers." I leaned my body against his.

Chris grabbed the cooler and the blanket. "Jump on my back," he laughed. Squatting down, I jumped on his back and wrapped my legs around his waist. With my arms around his neck, he carried me to the truck.

On arriving back at the house, Chris came around to my door to open it. Jumping down, he put his arm around me and walked me up to the house. "Want to come in?"

"Yes," he responded and pulled me in and kissed me. "But not tonight."

"Okay." I was disappointed but knew tonight wasn't the best night to be our first night together. "Just so you know, if you keep kissing me like that, I may never leave town."

"I'll keep that in mind," Chris said and kissed me again. Now I really wished he wasn't such a good guy. I needed a cold shower.

Chapter 17

I was glad Kathy was back at the bakery and I could sleep in again. Getting ready in the morning, I made myself some scrambled eggs and sat down to call my mom. She had been working at the mission store for over a month. She worked every Tuesday and Thursday with the same group of women. She was making new friends and had decided to join a Friday night euchre group. I was happy she was doing so well. I told her all about the beach, meeting Cyndee and Lilly, and the concert in the park.

"What are your plans for coming home?" she asked when I told her Chris and I had our first fight.

"I'm not sure. I don't really have any plans right now. I know I need to start figuring things out. I like staying at the farmhouse, and Kathy said I could stay as long as I need to. Did I tell you I have a set of hummingbirds that come to my feeder? I can watch them when I sit on the porch swing."

Our conversation was interrupted when I could hear my mom's doorbell. "Can you hold on a second?" she asked as I could hear her walking to answer the door. I tried to listen to see if I could tell who it was, but I didn't recognize the voices. "Hey, Melissa, I'm going to have to give you a call later. My friends are here, and we are heading to the casino today on a bus trip. I'm using Dad's stash. He would like that."

"Oh, okay. Call me if you win big." I hung up a little shocked but excited for my mom. For so long, she took care of my dad and wasn't able to go and do fun things. I felt a little better knowing that she didn't need me as much as I thought she did. She was living her life for the first time in a long time. Maybe I needed to just concentrate on living my own life for a while too. There wasn't really any need to hurry back to her.

"Hi honey." Kathy waved at me as I entered the bakery. She was baking bread. "It feels so good to be back to work."

"I am sure the customers are glad you are back too. I don't think my bread was quite up to par."

"That's because I always leave out one ingredient from the recipe. That way, if I die and someone else uses my recipes, their bread will never live up to mine. It's about pride, Melissa. I want the people of this community to forever say, 'No bread was ever as good as Kathy's.' Stick around, and I might tell you what it is, but don't get your hopes up."

"That's dirty, Kathy," I said as I headed back to do the dishes. "Just plain dirty." I could hear her laughing as I started the dish water.

The next couple of hours flew by. Kathy and I sat at the table and drank some coffee, and I filled her in on meeting Cyndee at the beach. I told her about Chris and I having our first fight.

"Oh, I think I'm to blame for that. I told Chris that you might be leaving town and he better decide what he wants before it was too late. I knew as soon as I told him that I pushed him too far. He left my house and must have headed right over to see you."

"Yeah, he kind of yelled at me. Well not really yelled, but was just accusing me of planning on leaving without saying anything to him. He has issues, obviously. We worked it out though. We went to the concert last night. Unfortunately, I hadn't eaten all day at the beach, and the wine coolers went right to my head."

"Let me guess. Chris tucked you into bed and left without taking advantage of the situation. Darn that boy."

"Nailed it. Probably good though. I am really starting to fall for him, and I want everything to be perfect when he does stay over." Kathy stood up and shook her head. It wasn't the exciting story she wanted. As I walked home, I made a plan for the day. I needed to go to the hardware store and get more hummingbird food and return my library book.

Chapter 18

After cleaning up, I grabbed the air pump from the front closet and filled up the air in the bike tires. Then I headed into town. It was good to be back on the bike, my hair blowing in the wind. As I rode past Chris's house, I noticed a small car parked next to his truck. I looked but couldn't see anyone in the field. I debated stopping by but decided to stop on the way home instead.

Leaning my bike against the wall, I walked to the hardware store. Ruger was lying in the sun by the door. He raised his eyes to look at me when I walked in, but didn't stand up. "How are you doing today, buddy?" I said as I reached down to pet him. He took a deep breath and shut his eyes. The smell of popcorn was so inviting that I walked right up to the machine and grabbed a paper bag. I was filling it up when the old woman came over to me. "Looks like you made a friend. Couldn't stay away from our popcorn, could you?"

"It is the best in town, but I need to get some more hummingbird food." She walked me over to the aisle and showed me the different kinds. I decided on the red food because that is what I used last time and the birds seemed to like it.

"Look at these new squirrel feeders I got in stock this week." She pulled up this tiny 6" picnic table with a nail in the middle. "You take one of these dried corn cobs and stick it on the nail. When the squirrels come and eat it, it looks like they are sitting at the table, eating lunch."

"That is amazing." I laughed. "I'll take it."

She gave me a small bag of dried corn cobs. "You are going to need these too."

"Perfect. Do you know if Cyndee is working today? I forgot to check if her sign was on when I parked my bike."

"Yep, that girl works every day. Just head up those stairs, and her shop is at the top. Why don't I just take your basket up to the counter and you can pay on the way out?"

She took my basket, and I headed up the stairs. At the top of the stairs was a glass door with a picture of a grim reaper holding a curling iron. Curl Up and Dye was written in black on the door. I could see Cyndee inside working on a client. I debated if I should go in or stop back at another time. She spotted me and waved me in. As I walked in, Cyndee said, "I'll be with you in a second. I'm just finishing up."

I sat on the green velvet couch. A glass table sat in front of it, covered with hairstyle magazines. Next to the couch was a huge old trunk filled with toys. The way the couch sat, I could look out the window and look over town. Cyndee was far enough away that I couldn't hear her conversation, but could see her working.

As the customer walked out, Cyndee walked over to me. "Hey. I'm glad you came in."

"Yeah, it was really nice to talk with you and Lilly at the beach the other day. I thought I would stop in to see your shop. I thought Lilly might be here too." Cyndee sat down on top of the chest next to me.

"My parents took her to the zoo. When she isn't at school, she is usually in here with me. That is why I have so many toys in the chest for her to play with. All my clients know that she is going to be here, and it doesn't bother them. If I get a new client and they don't understand, they usually don't come back. It works out for everyone that way. It is nice for my clients that have kids too. They don't worry about having to find a babysitter. They know I will understand."

"Well it's nice you got a break today. Perfect time for me to come in."

"I don't have another appointment for a while either, unless I get a walk-in. I live in the apartment next door, which makes it super convenient. I can have a 6 a.m. appointment or a 9 p.m. appointment, and it's not really that big of a deal. I can run home and do all my chores and just come back. Usually it's the old farmers who like to come in at 6 a.m. They come into town to grab a cup of coffee at that store and sit and talk with their buddies and usually come here first. They are also the ones that don't make appointments." I shook my head and nodded as she talked.

"It's nice your parents have Lilly for the day."

"Yeah, they help me out a lot. When I came home pregnant, they weren't very happy, to say the least. They pretty much told me, 'You made this bed. You can lie in it.' So I had to figure things out fast. Betty, the lady that owns the hardware store, kind of took me under her wings. Her husband remodeled this space up here so I would have a place to live. Then she added on the shop for me after I finished beauty school. I used to work at the hardware store when I was in high school and dating Chris. She never had any kids, and I was the closest thing she ever had.

"Lilly calls them Nana and Papa. They love her like she is blood. I could never do enough to thank them for all their help.

"After Lilly was born, though, my parents stopped being mad at me. It's hard to be angry when you see the good that came out of a terrible situation. You know what I mean?"

I nodded, "Does Lilly see much of her dad?"

"Ha!" Cyndee let out a fake, loud laugh. "No, he doesn't even know about her, and I'd like to keep it that way. He is a total loser that I met at a bar one night. We barely knew each other's names. I was young and stupid, and he was old and an alcoholic. We both got what we wanted that night and never talked to each other again," Cyndee continued, scrunching her nose, showing disappointment with herself. "I really hurt Chris badly. Chris is the best man I have ever met. He just wasn't what I wanted at the time. I wish I could have done things differently, but I will never regret having Lilly. She is the only good thing that I have ever had in my life. I just regret that she doesn't have a real dad. I barely even date. Most men my age don't want a premade family."

"Oh, I don't know if that's true. You just haven't met the right person yet. Chris told me he just wants the best for you."

"Yeah, I feel the same. So how are you guys?"

"We are good. He mostly just works a lot, so we haven't had a ton of time together. Plus, I was working a lot at the bakery, covering for Kathy, but she's back now. I guess I am just trying to figure things out. At some point, I am going to run out of money and have to get a full-time job again."

"Don't rush into that. Working is overrated," Cyndee laughed as she gave me a little push.

"Yeah, but I do like to eat. A lot. I just need to figure something out. It's nice to talk to someone more my age though. Poor Kathy is stuck listening to me every day. And I hate to talk to her about Chris because he is like a son to her. Plus, I sometimes feel like she is pressuring him to date me."

"Oh, if you haven't figured it out, no one pressures Chris into anything. That man is always on the up and up. That is kind of why it didn't work out for us. I was looking for more of a bad boy than an angel. What a mistake that was."

"Sometimes I wish he wasn't so honorable, if you know what I mean."

"Oh I know what you mean." We laughed.

Just then, the door opened, and an old man walked in. "Have time for a high and tight?"

I stood up and headed toward the door. As I opened it, Cyndee said, "Thanks for stopping in, Melissa. I'll tell Lilly you said hello."

I waved and headed downstairs toward the register to check out. Ruger hadn't moved. Betty rang me up and handed me my hummingbird food and my new squirrel picnic table. "I can't wait to set up my new feeder. Thanks, Betty." It was nice to finally know her name.

As I was loading the basket, I looked up and waved to Cyndee. I couldn't tell if she could see me or not, but I figured she was probably looking out the window. Jumping onto the seat, I headed toward the library.

Chad was working the front desk, checking in new books. He had set aside a few books that were returned from the author I liked. He was good at his job. Grabbing the books, I checked myself out and headed back home. Riding past Chris's house, the small car was still in his driveway. I debated if I should stop in but just decided I would call him later that afternoon.

Chapter 19

The first thing I did when I got home was set up the squirrel picnic table. On the opposite side of the hummingbird feeder, I screwed the table onto the railing. Taking the dried corn out of the bag, I pushed it on top of the nail. Then I snapped a picture to send to my mom.

Heading inside, I decided to make myself a salami and cheese sandwich. Sitting down at the table, I called Chris. The phone rang, and my call was sent to voicemail. That was the first time Chris had rejected my call. Before I could even set the phone down, I received a text. "Can't talk now. I'll call you tonight."

Now my thoughts were racing. I wanted to drive by Chris's house again to see if I could see what was going on. I'm sure it was nothing, but I couldn't help but wonder. Maybe I should call Kathy or stop by the store and conveniently talk to Connie. One of them would know something, at least who owned the car. I decided that seemed a bit obsessive. I needed to just chill out. It was probably just farm business.

After my lunch, I decided to take a walk. I headed down the dirt road toward the farm with the cows. As I got toward the end of the road, the cows spotted me and started trotting toward the fence. "Well, hello, my friends," I said as they came near. Staying on the road, I continued, "Don't come visit me tonight. You just stay right here."

At the end of the road, I decided to head around the block. I was hoping that I could take three lefts and end up where I started. Forty-five minutes later, I was home, hot and tired. Looking at my phone, I checked my distance, 3.8 miles, and still no call back from Chris. I decided to grab some iced water and just relax on the porch for a while. As I was sitting there, I saw a police car go by, which seemed weird since that was the first time since I had been here that I had seen a cop, and I worked at a bakery. I smiled to myself. When another cop drove by, I got a little pit in my stomach. I decided to call Chris.

When he didn't answer, I decided I would jump in my truck and drive by his farm just to make sure he wasn't in some kind of farming accident or something. As I was driving up toward his barn, both police cars were in his driveway. One officer was talking to Chris and another to a small-framed woman with long blonde hair. As I parked, Chris looked over at me. He didn't wave or smile, which made me concerned. As I jumped out, I timidly walked over to where they were standing. "Hey, everything okay? What's going on?"

Chris just shook his head, and I took his signal to not get involved. I walked back to my truck and leaned against the hood, sitting on the front bumper. When the officer finished talking with Chris, he walked over to the other officer who was still talking with the woman. As they talked to her, I could tell she had been crying. Her face was red and swollen. Her eyes were blackened, and it looked like her nose had been broken. I watched as she straightened out her arms and showed bruises on her shoulders and wrists. She was beaten up pretty badly. One officer took notes while the other officer took pictures. Chris walked over to wait with me as the officers finished with the woman.

"What's going on? Are you okay? Who is that?" I drilled him with questions.

"That's my sister, Hannah. Her husband beat the crap out of her yesterday. When he passed out drunk, she was able to drive up here and get away." Looking at me directly in the eyes, I didn't recognize him. "I'm going to kill him," he whispered. He scared me at that moment because I believed him. I looked over as the cops were finishing up with her. "Would you mind if I fill you in later? She is in a bad spot right now."

"Of course," I said, squeezing his shoulder with my hand. We both stood up, and I got into the driver's seat. As I started backing out of the driveway, I saw the police officers and Hannah walking back to finish up with Chris. As I made eye contact with Hannah, she looked down and rubbed her forehead in an attempt to hide her face. I looked away quickly so she wouldn't feel embarrassed and left the driveway. I couldn't imagine what kind of man would ever hit a woman.

As I turned my truck off and pulled my keys out of the ignition, I realized my hands were shaking. Chris had scared me. Chris had a clear definition of right and wrong. Things with him were black or white; there were no gray areas. What had happened to Hannah was wrong. He was going to make it right. I believed him when he said he would kill Hannah's husband.

Lying in bed, I didn't sleep all night. All I could think about was Hannah and how frightened she must be. Her husband definitely needed to pay for what he did. I was all for him getting hit by a bus or getting some rare disease that would make him paralyzed from the neck down. I just didn't want Chris to go and do something stupid.

When the bakery light came through the window, I looked at the clock: 3:33. Every time my mom and I would see 333, we would say, "Father, Son, and Holy Spirit." It was something we said since I was little. I said a quick prayer for Hannah and Chris. Then I decided I would get up and head to the bakery early. I wasn't sleeping anyway.

Chapter 20

As I walked into the bakery, Kathy jumped. "You scared me, honey. I thought you might come in early today. I didn't think it would be this early though. I suppose you heard what's going on."

Putting on an apron, I turned on the oil on the doughnut fryer. "Well not really. I stopped in at Chris's place when the cops were there talking to Hannah. It looks like she was beat up pretty bad. Chris said he would call me last night, but he didn't. I am worried about what he might do next. He told me he was going to kill him."

"Well last time this happened, he almost did." Kathy started mixing the bread. "It was right after Hannah and Danny got married. Hannah and Danny dated for about a year. His family owns a construction company and has a house right on Lake Michigan. Danny liked to act like he had a lot of money. He would take Hannah on trips, out on his parents' boat, and he liked to party. He was a lot of fun. Hannah and Chris never got to do those kinds of things. Their parents were farmers. So when Danny came along, it was exciting for Hannah. The truth is, his parents had the money, not Danny. He liked to drink more than he liked to work. Danny was the type of person that could smooth-talk anyone, and Hannah fell hard for it. Chris never liked him. He saw right through his bull. He would say, 'I don't know what she sees in that wing nut.'

"After they were married, apparently, Hannah was tired of Danny drinking and not working. Well one day, she told him just that, and it ended up with him breaking her arm in a fight. Hannah had called Chris, crying. He raced over there and put such a beat down on Danny that he was hospitalized for a week. Danny's parents were worried about their reputation and how it would look for their business. They pressured Hannah into trying to work it out with

Danny. In return, he wouldn't press charges on Chris. Of course, Danny promised it would never happen again. After that, they gave Hannah and Danny a 'belated wedding gift' and sent them on a trip to Italy. It was more of a bribe rather than a gift. When they came back from Italy, Dann's parents had decided to open a branch of their construction business in Ohio. Hannah and Danny moved there and have barely come back even to visit, until now."

"That all sounds terrible." I fried the doughnuts as Kathy continued making the bread. "You don't think Danny will come up here and try to bring her back, do you?"

"Not if he likes breathing, but that boy is stupid and a drunk. He will probably call his parents to try to get them to help. It is not going to end well, trust me."

We worked the rest of the morning in silence. When the dishes were done, I grabbed myself a doughnut and some coffee and went to sit at the table. Chad stopped in on the way to the library and visited with Abby. They were whispering at the counter, obviously talking about Hannah. I am sure Chad heard the call on his fire department radio. I drank my coffee and watched as the customers came in. It was nice to see people come in just to visit with Kathy. I can see why she loved working here so much. When my coffee was done, I checked my phone. Still there was no call from Chris. I decided to head home and take a quick nap. I was feeling a little down today, and I thought a nap might revive my mood.

Chapter 21

A few days went by, and still there was no word from Chris. Finally, I decided to drive over to his house to see what was going on. Pulling up, Hannah's car was gone. I was a little relieved that Chris would be alone, although I prayed she didn't go back home. Knocking on the door, it took some time before it opened. I was surprised when Hannah answered.

"Oh, hi Hannah." Looking her over, her nose was still swollen. The swelling in her face had gone down, although her bruising was now a deep purple. "I'm Melissa, Chris's friend. I just wanted to check on you two and see how you are doing."

"Come on in. Chris took my car to Pete's to get an oil change and the brakes looked at. To be honest, I think he just needed some fresh air." Walking over to the kitchen table, I sat down. She grabbed an apple pie off the counter and two plates. "I made some pie this morning. I am trying to keep busy." She avoided eye contact, obviously trying to hide her face. Upon sitting down, she cut us both a piece and sat down across from me.

"How are you holding up?" I really didn't know what to say.

"I'm okay. Chris is helping me with everything. I don't know how much Chris has told you, but we went down to the courthouse to file a personal protection order yesterday. Once Danny gets a copy of it, I don't know what he'll do." Just then, her phone rang. Looking at it, she clicked it off. "Danny has been calling me nonstop." Her eyes were filled with tears. "This is my own fault. I should have left him the first time he hurt me, but I was young and stupid. I let his parents talk me into staying. He promised me he would change, and I wanted so badly to believe him. Quite honestly, I'm so embarrassed. I'm embarrassed I fell for his sweet talk and lies. I am embarrassed I let him hurt me. I'm embarrassed that I have a terrible marriage and have to come crawling home to my brother to save me."

I didn't know what to say. To be honest, I had never been in this type of situation before. "You shouldn't be embarrassed. He is the one that should be embarrassed. What are your next steps?"

"I'm not sure. I need to file for divorce. I don't even know where to get started."

"I will help in any way I can. I know it's weird because you don't know me, but I don't really know too many people here. It will be nice to have another person to talk to." Trying to change the subject, I asked, "Would you like to maybe go to the beach with me? It might be nice for you to get out of the house for a while. We can stop in town and pick up some snacks and just spend a couple of hours soaking up the sun." I took another bite of pie and tried to give her time to think.

"I don't know." She pushed away her piece of pie. "That does really sound great, but I don't have a swimsuit. Plus, I don't really want to see anyone."

"You don't need to see anyone. We can sit alone and away from everyone. I can call Cyndee to see if you can borrow one of her suits. Come on, I think it will be good for your mental health just to get a break. We can leave Chris a note. Come on, let's go now before you get a chance to change your mind."

Her eyes lit up a little. Grabbing a piece of paper and a pen, she wrote, "Going to the beach with Melissa." "Let's go." I grabbed the plates and put them in the sink. "Chris can get these when he gets home." We laughed and ran to my truck. As I drove us to my house, I called Cyndee to get Hannah a swimsuit.

After changing into my suit and grabbing the cooler, we headed to the hardware store to pick up the swimsuit from Cyndee. As we pulled up, Cyndee was at the front door waving us in. I looked at Hannah, "You stay here. I'll run up and get the swimsuit."

"Hannah doesn't want to see anyone," I explained to Cyndee. "Well she's going to see me because I'm coming with you girls. Give me a second to change, and I'll be right out. Here is her suit and a towel. Just have her change in the truck."

Running back to the truck, I handed Hannah her swimsuit and towel through her open window. "Go ahead and change here." I turned my back to her and kept talking. "Cyndee is coming with us, I hope you don't mind. She really did allow me to say no."

Before she had the chance to answer, Cyndee was jumping in the back seat. "I brought some wine coolers. We just need to stop at the store for some ice."

Hannah turned around and looked at her. "Thanks for the suit."

"I have anything you need while you are back in town. If you want, later on, you can go shopping in my closet and pick out some clothes. Now let's get out of here before someone stops in for a haircut."

Driving over to the store, I jumped out. "You guys wait here. I will be right back." As I headed into the store, I could hear Cyndee's phone ringing. "Turn that phone off. We are going to have a stress-free afternoon."

A few minutes later, I came back to the truck and handed the bag of ice to Cyndee. "Can you fill up the cooler? I didn't know what you guys liked for snacks, so I got pretzels, chips, and tons of different kinds of candy."

The next couple of hours at the beach were great. I heard stories of how Cyndee and Hannah hung out together. Cyndee filled Hannah in on all the local gossip. I told her how Chris had rescued me when my car broke down on the expressway. We talked about Kathy's heart and the bakery. I told them how Kathy's left out ingredients on her bread recipes. We all laughed, ate candy, and drank our coolers. Not a word was mentioned about Danny, and Hannah seemed to forget her worries for a little while. Finally, Cyndee said she had to get back to the shop before Lilly got back from a friend's house.

As we headed back, we all laughed and listened to music. I dropped off Cyndee first. "I'm not coming over to your farm, but come by my shop any time or just give me a buzz." Opening the door, she ran into the store, never looking back or waiting for a response.

Driving away, I looked at Hannah and asked, "Is it weird for you hanging out with her?"

"No. I knew it would never work out with Chris and her. Chris wouldn't listen to me when I tried to warn him that they were just different types of people. Just like I wouldn't listen to Chris when he told me Danny was a piece of crap. Sometimes you just have to learn for yourself."

As I pulled into the driveway, Chris came running out. "Where the hell have you been? I have been trying to call you all afternoon."

Jumping out, Hannah looked at me with her mouth open. "We went to the beach. I turned off my phone because Danny kept calling. I'm so sorry. We did leave you a note."

I tried to interrupt, "It's my fault, Chris. I just thought we could escape for the day and not think about things." Chris didn't even look at me.

"I got home from Pete's, and there are two plates in the sink. I thought you left with Danny. I didn't see any note. What the hell! You can't do this to me. I almost went to Danny's parents' house."

"I'm so sorry." Hannah's eyes were filled with tears.

Chris took a deep breath. "I was just worried something happened to you."

Opening the door, I looked at Hannah. "I guess I'll talk to you later. Call me if you need anything."

Jumping in my truck, I left without talking to Chris. He was pissed, and I knew it. It was probably best to just talk with him after he cooled down. As I pulled into my driveway, I received a text from Hannah. "My phone's back on. Oops. Thanks for today. It was the best day I have had in years."

Reading it made me feel better. Chris might be mad, but at least, Hannah was okay. As I headed into the house, a little squirrel was sitting at his picnic table, eating his corn. I took a picture and sent it to my mom. I knew she would think it was hysterical. Walking straight to the kitchen, I grabbed a mug. I needed a margarita.

Chapter 22

After taking a nice relaxing bath, I threw on some cotton shorts and a tank top, grabbed my book, and headed out to the porch swing. I had barely sat down when Chris pulled into the driveway. As he got out, I looked him over. I liked the way he looked in his jeans and T-shirt, his baseball hat pulled over his forehead, with his thick crease between his eyes. I wondered if he got that from squinting in the sun or having the burden of the world on his shoulders. His arms were dark from the sun and toned from working on the farm. His hands were thick and calloused. He was a man's man. He was rugged and strong and made me feel safe. He saw me sitting on the swing. We didn't say anything, but we just watched each other.

Walking up to the swing, he sat down. He reached over and put his hand on my leg. When I leaned into him, he put his arm around my shoulders. I think that was his way of apologizing for screaming earlier. "Thanks for taking care of Hannah today."

"You're welcome. I thought it would be good for her to get out and soak up the sun. Vitamin D always makes things seem better."

"Well it definitely helped her. When I went inside to grab some dinner, she was asleep on the couch." Chris squeezed me in tighter. "She hasn't slept since she got home. I can hear her at night crying or just walking around. This has taken a lot out of her. She used to laugh and be a little crazy. Now she is just sad and broken. Today was good for her."

"We laughed a lot. Cyndee came with us too. They were telling stories about high school and reliving the days when they both were a little more carefree." I snuggled tighter to him. "So what's next?"

"I'm taking her to town tomorrow to file for divorce. Dan is also going to be served the restraining order, if he hasn't already. Then shit is going to hit the fan. If he isn't already on his way up here, he will be soon. He has been calling her nonstop. Now his parents have started calling her too. He better not step foot on my property, or I will put a bullet in his head."

"Chris, that is the last thing that Hannah needs, you killing her husband and going to jail for life. Then what will she have?" I answered my one question. "Nothing! After what happened last time, I doubt he will go to your house. But if you are worried he is going to come look for her, maybe we need to have her stay with me. We could park her car at Pete's so he won't know where to find her. We just need to make sure she is somewhere safe until this whole mess is over." I knew Chris wasn't much of a drinker, but I handed him my margarita. "Want some? It tastes so good."

"I'd rather just taste it on your lips." He leaned down and kissed me. It was a good kiss, a long, nice, make-your-stomach-churn kind of kiss.

As he pulled away, I whispered, "I have a whole bottle if you want to keep kissing me like that." He smiled and kissed me again and again.

I didn't want him to stop. I wanted him to take my hand and lead me inside. Instead, he looked at me and said, "I better head home and check on Hannah. I just don't know if Dan will show up or not."

"You know you could always just call her." I didn't want the night to end.

"I wish. I turned her phone off before I left. I didn't want Dan or his idiot parents calling her all night long. I just wanted her to get some sleep. Just so you know, I don't want to leave. I really, really don't want to leave." He gave me that crooked smile that I have grown to love.

"You know, I'm going to stop asking soon." I raised my eyebrows at him.

"No, you won't." He laughed. He was right, and he knew it. Standing up, he suggested, "What do you think about having a cookout on your firepit tomorrow night? We could invite Kathy and maybe a few other people. Then Hahhan could just stay here after that."

"Sounds perfect. I will go into town tomorrow after work and pick up some hot dogs and hamburgers." Before he left, he pulled me in tight, his arms around my hips. As he held me, I knew I was falling in love with him.

Chapter 23

The next morning at the bakery, Kathy and I decided who we would invite to the cookout. We decided to keep the group small. "Forget making hot dogs and hamburgers. That's too much work. You should make hobo pies to cook directly over the firepit." She wrote down what I would need: aluminum foil, potatoes, carrots, red onions, and hamburger. "All you have to do is cut up all the vegetables into little squares. Rip out large squares of foil, one for each person. Then add a hamburger patty to each square, cover the patty with all the vegetables, add some Lawry's seasoning, salt and pepper, and a tab of butter. Then fold the foil into a little pocket. It's super easy. I'll bring some pies."

"Got it. I think I will also buy marshmallows so we can make s'mores. I was thinking about inviting Cyndee and Lilly. Do you think that would be okay? Hannah and I had a lot of fun with Cyndee the other day. I just don't want it to be awkward for Chris."

"You know what, honey? I think it's time we all moved on from something that happened a long time ago. If it makes Hannah happy, it will make Chris happy. And I think Lilly would love to have some s'mores."

Jumping in the truck, I headed directly to the grocery store. I thought about stopping by the farm to pick up Hannah, but I remembered she was at the lawyer's office with Chris. Thinking about Hannah, I thought about how much strength she had. She was embarrassed about the situation, but I didn't see her as a failure. I saw her as a strong woman who was able to get out of a bad situation. My thoughts turned to Danny. I drove by the farm slowly, looking to see if there was a strange car in the driveway or a man lurking around. I was worried for Hannah's safety. No man that is worth anything would ever hit a woman. By now, he probably had received his personal protection order to stay away from Hannah. From what Kathy and Chris had told me about Danny, I was sure he wasn't going to stay away.

Walking in the grocery store, Connie was working the candy counter. A group of high school girls were drinking strawberry shakes and giggling. It made me think about the stories Cyndee and Hannah were telling at the beach. For a minute, I missed being young. "Need more candy today, Melissa? I think my sales have doubled since you moved in town." The high school girls all looked at each other, then looked at me up and down in a judging way. It was at that moment that I remembered what a loser I was in high school and was glad I was older now.

"I just need some Hershey's minis for making s'mores. Can you get me a mix of light and dark chocolate? You know they say dark chocolate helps with stress. That's how I justify eating so much." The girls at the counter whispered between themselves. Connie ignored my comment and just handed me my bag. "Thanks, Connie. You're awesome."

She looked at me shocked, as if she had never received a compliment. "Thanks. I'll make sure I keep the candy stocked for you." Then she looked at the girls, and they all laughed.

Whatever, I thought, thinking she probably needed a nicotine break to help her be nice. Then I headed to the produce department. Getting out the list Kathy wrote, I checked each item off. Then I got some Vernors, juice boxes for Lilly, and wine coolers. If Cyndee was coming, she would definitely want some wine coolers.

After I loaded up the car, I drove to the hardware store to talk to Cyndee. I pushed the door open, sliding Ruger's limp body across the floor. "No need to get up and move, Ruger." I reached down and petted him. His eyes opened in disgust, letting me know I interrupted his deep sleep.

"Hi, Betty." I waved as I headed toward the stairs. Then smelling the popcorn, I turned around to grab a bag. "You know I can't come in without having some of the best popcorn in town." Betty's eyes lit up with pride.

"How do the squirrels like their picnic table?"

Going over to her, I pulled up the picture I had taken to send to my mom. "They love it. I sent this picture to my mom, and now she thinks we are all crazy."

"We are crazy, but we're a good crazy. It's better than being boring." She wasn't lying.

"That's true," I said. "You know, just so you know, Cyndee told me how much you mean to her. She is glad Lilly has such a great Nana and Papa."

"We love them too. You know, Melissa, I think you are bringing a lot of healing to this town. I am really glad you are here." Both of our eyes filled up with tears.

We hugged, and I pointed toward the stairs. "I am going up now, before I totally break down into a crying mess. You know, I miss my mom too. You might need to adopt me for a little while too." I didn't look back, but I heard her blow her nose. I knew she was a crying mess now.

Cyndee was sitting on the green couch, reading a *People* magazine. "You and Lilly got any plans for tonight? I am having a few people over for a cookout tonight."

"I'm not sure." She gave me a kind of cringe look. "Don't you think it will be weird with you and me and Chris there?"

"No, I don't think it will be weird at all. Plus, Hannah needs you there. I bought juice boxes and s'mores for Lilly. Come on, you're like one of my few friends. Please? For Lilly. I bought wine coolers. If you don't come, I'll drink all the wine coolers. And if I drink all the wine coolers, there is no way Chris will spend the night, you know, because he's noble."

"Okay, okay, I'll come, but just because you need me to drink all the booze."

"Great, see you around six." Heading out, I thought about what Betty said. It made me really happy.

Chapter 24

I was at the sink peeling potatoes when Chris and Hannah showed up. Chris sneaked up behind me and put his hands around my waist and his chin on my shoulder, pinning my hips to the counter, "Hey there, good looking," he whispered in my ear and kissed my neck, making me wish it was just going to be us tonight.

"Come on now." I laughed, pretending I wanted him to stop. "I've got work to do. So either grab a peeler or get out of this kitchen."

Backing up, he said, "No, thanks. I'll go work on the fire. Hannah is in the backyard setting up some chairs. But before I head out, I have something for you." He headed out toward the front door and came back. "I want you to keep this here." He held up a shotgun and tried to hand it to me.

"Why would I take that? I wouldn't even know how to use it." I shook my head no.

"If Hannah is going to stay here, you need to have something to keep you guys safe, in case Danny shows up." Holding it up, he pointed it away from me. "All you have to do is click the safety off, point, and pull the trigger. He showed me the red safety button on the side of the gun. "It's loaded. I'll put it next to your bed."

"I don't feel comfortable taking that," I said, continuing to shake my head.

"I'll take you out later this week, and we can practice. It's no use having it unless you are comfortable with it."

"Okay, that's a deal." Picking up the shotgun, Chris started out of the kitchen to bring the shotgun upstairs. "Hey, at least, I can finally tell Kathy that I got you in my bedroom." Shaking his head, he left the room.

Turning back to the sink, I got back to peeling the potatoes. Hannah soon came in and joined me. Grabbing a knife, she started cutting them up. Her black eyes were healing, just a slight green around her cheek bones. "How'd it go at the lawyers?"

"It went fine. It is all kind of stressful, but I am ready to be done with Danny. He has left me at least thirty messages and texts. I don't even listen to them. His parents have called me too. They want me to forgive him. They are trying to make me feel guilty like it's my fault. Every time the phone rings, I get all upset. I am glad I at least have the divorce paperwork started."

"Well hopefully this will all be over soon, and you can start new. It will be so nice having you here with me. It will be like having a sleepover."

"It will be nice to get away from Chris for a little while. We are starting to get on each other's nerves. He won't let me have two seconds alone." Just as she said that, Chris walked in the room.

"Did I just hear you telling Mel what an awesome brother I am?"

"Exactly. Like I was saying, Melissa, he is so wonderful. And all he talks about is this great girl he is dating."

"Don't tell Mel that. She might get jealous." Coming over to me, he gave me a quick kiss. I pretended to reject him, but he pulled me in.

"You're very funny. Now get out of here and go get the fire going." Heading out to the backyard, I could hear him mumbling about having to do man's work.

Hannah looked at me and rolled her eyes. "He complains, but he loves every second of this. Even with everything that's going on with me, this is the happiest I have seen Chris in a long, long time."

"You know, after my dad died, all I wanted to do was get away and travel. I didn't want to have a care or worry in the world. But now I care about Chris so much, and I worry about you. And I am so happy too. Not what I had planned for my summer, but better than I could have ever imagined." She came over and hugged me.

"Hey, ladies! I'm here. The party can start now." Cyndee came busting into the kitchen. "Where are those wine coolers you promised me?"

Cyndee was rough, but it was kind of what I liked about her. You never really guessed what she was thinking because she would usually tell you. "They're in the fridge. Grab Hannah and me one too. Where is Lilly?"

Handing us the coolers, she cracked hers open and took a big swig. "She's in the back playing with fire. I am sure it's safe, right?" She smiled. "That kid is on my last nerve today. If I had to hear one more time about the dang s'mores, I would have lost it." She took another sip. "I'm gonna need a lot more of these to destress."

"We have plenty. And if you guys need to spend the night, you're welcome to." Just then, Kathy and Pete walked into the kitchen.

"Looks like the party's in here." Kathy began setting down the pies on the kitchen table. Pete opened the refrigerator door and put in a twelve-pack of Bud Lite, grabbing one out for him and Chris.

"Chris is out back with Lilly, working on the fire," I said, pointing outside. "Save yourself. It's getting rough in here."

"I know how to take a hint," he said, leaving out the back door.

Looking over at Kathy, I smiled. "You and Pete, eh? Why didn't I see that coming? Now I understand what you really meant when you said he was 'changing your oil.'"

"Don't read into it, Melissa. We have been old friends for a long time."

"Mmmmhhhmmm," I said, laughing. "Getting yourself a little hot tamale?"

Cyndee and Hannah joined in. "A little chimichanga, a little spicy burrito?" We all laughed. It was good to give it back to Kathy as she always gives it to us.

"When he said he liked your pillows, I thought he was talking about your blueberry pastries. I didn't know he was talking about your pillows." I pointed to her breasts.

"Stop it." She laughed. "But compared to others my age, they are the best pillows in town." She opened the refrigerator to grab herself a wine cooler.

"Grab out the hamburger too," I instructed her. "We have been talking and haven't finished making the hobo pies. You can help us now."

Cyndee grabbed the foil. "Is this everyone?" Hannah grabbed the knife and started cutting up the carrots and onions.

"No, Abby and Chad are coming too," I said. "And anyone else that stops by. Let's just make as many as we can with the burger that we have." Everyone agreed. We worked, laughed and drank, then headed outside with the hobo pies.

Chris and Pete were sitting by the fire, sharpening sticks to a point. Lilly would come back every so often with more sticks for roasting marshmallows. She would throw the little sticks directly onto the fire. I wondered, *Why is it that every man carries a pocket knife with him, just in case someone needs something cut or sharpened? You never see a woman grabbing a knife out of her purse.* I smiled to myself. *Except maybe Cyndee,* I thought. She probably has a knife in her purse, but I guessed it would be more like a switchblade. I looked over at her, and she was finishing her wine cooler. Standing up, she said, "I'm grabbing another drink. Who else needs one?"

"Can you grab me a beer?" Pete said, standing up. "Chris, can you help me move the picnic table over here?" As the guys moved the table over, Chad and Abby came through the back door.

I set the hobo pies on the table. "Dinner is ready to be cooked when the fire is ready." I looked at Chris and whispered, "I hope you don't mind that Cyndee is here."

"It's fine. Hannah and her have been good friends for a long time. The coals aren't quite ready yet." He grabbed one of his sticks and started poking at the fire. Chad and Abby set up their chairs in the circle around the fire and sat down. I took a deep breath and breathed in the smell of the campfire. Nothing smells better to a city girl than a campfire. Yes, what a perfect night.

After we finished eating, Kathy cut up the pies. Cyndee helped Lilly make some s'mores. Chad and Chris played cornhole. We all just sat near the fire and talked. Abby was talking to Hannah about veterinarian school. We all just listened to music until one by one, everyone started folding up their chairs and leaving. By midnight, it was just Hannah, Chris, and me.

"I think I'm going to head out," Chris said, standing up. "It's been a long day, and I have to get up early."

"Sounds good. Thanks for all your help tonight." He leaned in and kissed me. Hannah grabbed the chairs, and we headed toward the truck.

Grabbing her clothes out of the back seat, she thanked Chris. "We'll call you tomorrow."

Hannah and I went into the house. I showed her where her bedroom was. "If you don't mind," I said, smelling my hair. "I'm just going to wash the smoke out of my hair and go to bed."

"Sounds perfect. I'm exhausted." Hugging me, she said, "Thanks for letting me stay here. I didn't think about Danny once tonight." She went into her room and shut the door.

I took a quick shower and immediately went to bed. As I lay there, I listened as Hannah's bed creaked. I was hoping she would be able to get a good night's sleep. Looking out the bedroom door, I saw the shotgun and went over Chris's instructions in my head. "Safety off, point, pull the trigger." The thought of having to use it was terrifying. I hoped I would never have to use it.

Chapter 25

I was in the kitchen making coffee when Hannah came downstairs. "Want a cup?" I asked.

"Yes. It smells so good." Once we both had coffee, we headed out to the porch swing. "This is so nice being here."

"I know. I love it. I usually just sit out here and watch the hummingbirds and squirrels. I have to go into work in a little bit. What are your plans for today?" I didn't want to be like Chris and not give her any space, but I did worry that Danny or his parents might show up.

"A couple of my high school friends are going to pick me up, and we are heading into the city. I need to stop at the mall and get some more clothes. When I left home, I left in a big hurry and only grabbed a few things to wear. I don't ever want to go back. So unless you don't want to see me in this outfit every other day for the rest of my life, I need to get some new clothes."

"Oh, that sounds fun. Do not forget Cyndee said you can borrow clothes from her too." I was glad she wasn't going to be alone. "What about your car? Did you drop it off at Pete's?"

"Yeah, we parked it behind this shop. Danny knows I am back, but at least, this way, he won't know where I am staying."

"That's true. He probably assumes you are staying with your brother, so I am glad you are here. I am going to go into town today and go grocery shopping. Do you need anything?"

"No, I'm good. I have really learned over the last couple of years to just not ask for anything for myself. As long as you keep making me coffee every morning, we should get along just fine. Oh, and I wouldn't complain if you brought home some doughnuts or blueberry pillows either." Then she looked at me and pointed to my boobs and said, "Kathy's pillows." Then we laughed hysterically.

Chapter 26

The bakery was hot and busy. Now that school was out, more and more kids would come in in the morning to pick up doughnuts. Kathy loved seeing everyone. She would often head up front and talk to people and then come back and tell me their story. I was just starting to figure out what it was like to know so many people all their lives. When I finished with all the cleanup, Kathy and I went to grab a coffee and to sit and talk at the picnic table.

"Thanks for coming last night. You know we were just teasing you about Pete, right." I knew she could take a little friendly harassment.

"Pete and I have been good friends for a very long time. After my husband died, he always made sure my car was always taken care of. He puts new tires on for the winter and does all the oil changes. He is a good man."

"Are you more than friends?" I smiled sideways at her.

"Melissa, at my age, a friend is the most important thing. We definitely have a bond. He knows how much I loved my husband. We can talk about him together, and he isn't hurt. I really like being with him. He is so kind and thoughtful." She smiled. "And he likes my pillows, I mean pastries." We laughed, "How about Chris? Anything new with you two?"

"We are good. He just has a lot going on right now with Hannah and Danny. Hannah said he is overwhelmed with worry about her. Did I tell you he brought over a shotgun yesterday in case Danny shows up?"

"That doesn't surprise me. He wants to make sure you can protect yourself."

"We are supposed to go out and practice shooting. I have never shot anything in all my life."

"Well you definitely need to practice. Chris is an expert. He loves to hunt. He will show you everything you need to know. It is just for safety, I doubt you will ever have to use it, but you never know. Danny is a fool. How is Hannah holding up?"

"She is doing okay. Chris took her to a lawyer, and they have started the paperwork for the divorce. I am not sure how it all works, but once Danny is served the papers, I doubt he will be very happy."

"That's the truth," she said, standing up. "Well I better get back at it."

Heading to the counter, I stopped to see Abby. "Thanks for coming last night. Did you guys have fun?"

"Yes, it was so fun. Chad said he smoked Chris in cornhole. Thanks for the invite."

"Any time. If you see Chad today, thank him for picking out some good books for me. That boy knows a good romance novel when he sees one. Maybe he is reading them and getting some good tips." Abby's face got red. *Oh no*, I thought. *Kathy is rubbing off on me.* Trying to quickly change the subject, I asked, "Can you get me a couple of cream-filled doughnuts? I promised Hannah I would bring some home."

When I got home, I decided I would make a list before heading to the store. I would probably need to drive the truck now that I was shopping for two. I would need to get more coffee and margaritas and definitely candy, you know, the essentials, I thought.

Heading into town, I looked when I drove past Chris's farm. Chris was on the tractor on the back part of his acreage. I beeped when I drove by even though I knew he wouldn't hear me. I drove directly to the store and parked out front. Heading in, I decided to ignore Connie and head right back to get my groceries. My day was going well, and I didn't really want to deal with her negativity. I shopped slowly, walking up and down every aisle, making sure I got enough food for the week. As I shopped, I thought a lot about Chris and Hannah. Eventually I would have to figure out what I was going to do. I couldn't just stay at the farmhouse and pretend this was my life. Although my mom was getting along well without me, I felt as though I still needed to be home. I knew I needed to start thinking about making a plan for what would happen after this summer.

When I had all my groceries, I headed to the candy counter. "Hi, Connie. Can I get some Good and Plenties, some firewalls, and some sour gummy worms?" I decided to mix it up a little today. "How's your day going?" I asked in an attempt to keep her from drilling me with questions. I hoped to just hurry to the checkout.

"Another crazy week it seems, but you should know how that is. It's like you've been a magnet for activity ever since you got in town. First with Chris, then with Kathy's heart attack, and now with Hannah." She really knew how to get me fired up.

I waited for my candy without acknowledging her comment. When she finally handed it to me, I only responded, "I'm ready to check out now. I'll meet you at the register." Heading over, I wanted to scream. No matter how hard I had tried to be nice, she always seemed to have something rude to say.

As she rang me up, I avoided eye contact and decided against making small talk. I wasn't sure why she didn't like me or why she always had to say some smart remark, but she wasn't going to use me for gossip or suck the life out of me today. She finished up by saying, "Have a good week." I was sure she didn't mean it.

Leaving, I tried to shake the negativity off. I decided I would drive through town and see if there were any other shops that I could explore. At the end of the main street, I noticed an empty building. It looked as though at some point, it had been a feed mill. I thought it looked like the perfect spot for Abby to start her veterinarian office. As I passed The Brown Trout, I noticed that the parking lot was already filled with work trucks, obviously a hot spot for local construction workers. I wondered if they had weekly lunch specials too. The Friday night fish fry was so fun that I had been wanting to go back. Maybe I would see if Chris would like to go there again sometime, or maybe I could meet Hannah or Cyndee there for lunch.

Just then, my phone started buzzing. Picking it up, it was Chris. "I was just thinking about you. Were your ears ringing?"

"Hopefully you were thinking of something good. What are you girls doing today?"

"I only think good thoughts about you, and it's just me today. Hannah went to the mall with some high school friends. So I ran to the grocery store to get the week's shopping done. I just drove by The Brown Trout. They must have a pretty good lunch menu because the place was packed. I was thinking we could meet there for lunch, or maybe Cyndee, Hannah, and I could go."

"You don't want to go there during the week in the summer. It is always filled with riffraff from local construction projects. The crews usually start work early and end early. Then they spend the rest of the afternoon drinking. Sometimes it can get pretty rough. I don't want to go with the hottest girl in town and have to fist fight all the wing nuts that hit on you. Friday nights are more the family crowd and the only days to go during the summer. Anyway, since Hannah is gone, what are you doing this afternoon?"

"I don't really have anything planned. I just have to get home and take care of these groceries." I hoped he would want to come over for a little loving.

"Well how about I pick you up in an hour, and we can practice shooting that shotgun."

"Sounds like a plan. Should I wear something sexy?" I hoped he would take the hint.

He ignored my comment. "Okay, see you soon."

He hung up, and I rushed home to take care of the groceries. Then I headed upstairs to change my clothes. What do you wear to a shooting? Camouflage seemed like the right answer, but of course, I didn't have anything. I decided on khaki shorts, a T-shirt, and a baseball cap. I grabbed the gun from behind the door and carried it downstairs. It was a lot longer than I thought it would be. It was a lot heavier too. I wasn't confident I could handle it if Danny showed up. I definitely doubted my ability to shoot a person, even a terrible one.

Chapter 27

When Chris pulled up, I opened the door and placed the gun on the front porch, leaning against the house. I waved hello and headed back inside to get the bag of gummy worms. I wasn't sure how long we were going to be shooting, but I wanted to make sure I didn't starve to death.

When I got back to the porch, Chris was putting the gun in a case. "Ready?" he asked. He grabbed me by the waist and pulled me in for a kiss.

"Where are we going?" I asked, assuming that we were going to some firing range or gun club.

"We're just going to my house. I have a set up at the back of my property."

At the back of Chris's property were a table and a bench. Chris set the shotgun on the table. He took it out of its case and took a box of shotgun shells out of his vest. At the other end of the range were a huge pile of sand and some wooden targets, with paper circles stapled to them. "Sit down," he said. "The gun is already loaded. Make sure you only point the gun down range. Never point the gun at anything or anyone unless you plan on shooting it." He was very serious. I knew better than to joke with him. "Put these on." He handed me a pair of safety glasses and earmuffs." I put on the glasses but only held onto the earmuffs so I could listen to his instructions.

Putting the gun in my hands, he pointed. "This is the safety. The gun won't shoot if the safety is on. You don't want to click it off until you are ready to shoot. Click it off with your thumb." I did what he said.

"Isn't there supposed to be something I look through?" I asked because that is what you see in every sniper movie.

"This gun doesn't have a scope, just look down the end of the gun at the bead at the end of the barrel. Point where you want to shoot, and pull the trigger."

"Should I shoot now?" I asked nervously.

"Wait a second. In a protection situation, you won't have time to aim. So just point and pull the trigger. The shell is filled with little BBs that shoot out in a wide spread, so instead of one little entrance hole, you'll have a wide spray of BBs. So you want to just point the gun and shoot at the center mass."

"Got it," I said. Taking off my baseball hat, I put on the ear-muffs. I looked at Chris for his okay. When he nodded his head, I pulled the gun up, double-checked the safety with my thumb, and looked down the barrel. I pointed the bead at the black circle in the middle of the target and pulled the trigger. Even with the earmuffs on, the noise made my heart pound. Looking at the target, I could see a large spread of holes. "I hit it," I said excitedly, pulling off my earmuffs so I could hear him tell me how great I did. Rubbing my shoulder, I continued, "I didn't know it would kick so bad."

"You need to keep it tight to your shoulder. You did good though." It was not exactly the rave review I was looking for, but he was all business. "Now you need to rack the slide." He continued with his instructions, "So take your hand and pull back the slide."

"Is that this?" I asked, putting my hand underneath the gun?

"Yes, pull it back. When you do, the old shell will eject, and a new shell will load. There are two more bullets in the gun. This gun holds three. You shot one. You just loaded another one. After you shoot again, you will have one more shot. Let's go again. Remember to keep it tight to your shoulder."

I went over the instructions in my head, *Double-check the safety, point, shoot, and rack the slide.* I shot two more times and handed the gun to Chris. "Do you want to keep going?" he asked.

He loaded three more shells into the gun, and I shot all three. "I think that is good for today. I think my shoulder might be bruised. That was hard," I said, handing him the empty gun and dropping my arms to my side. "My arms hurt." He laughed. "Would it be okay if

I take a picture of the target? My mom will never believe me when I tell her I went shooting."

Chris set down the gun on the table, and we walked down the range. I was kind of skipping in excitement. "That was kind of exciting. I've never done anything like that before."

"Well, hopefully, you will never have to use it." Chris's words brought me back to reality. When we got to the target, I took a picture but decided I wouldn't send it to my mom. I didn't want to have to explain why I was learning to shoot. I could show her the pictures when I was back home, and Danny was just someone who was once married to a friend.

Chris reloaded the gun and put it back in the case. While driving back to the house, Chris told me he had more work to do. I listened as I finished off the bag of gummy worms. I was a little relieved because I really just wanted to spend the rest of the afternoon relaxing on the swing with my book.

Chapter 28

When we got back to the house, I took the gun back upstairs and set it behind the door. I was more comfortable with it but still hoped I would never have to use it. Grabbing my book from beside the bed, I headed downstairs to make myself a margarita.

Sitting on the swing, I took a huge sip of my drink. It was so refreshing on such a hot day. Plus, I needed it to help me with my nerves. It was kind of stressful learning to shoot. I think it was because Chris was so serious. I took another sip and looked up to check my bird feeder. It was gone. Jumping up, I looked around. I ran down the steps and saw it broken in one hundred pieces all over the grass. The syrup was spread everywhere. "Oh no," I said out loud. "What happened?" I thought it over in my head. I didn't think it was that windy. It couldn't have blown off. Maybe a squirrel knocked it down or a big bird hit it. I checked the hook when I was back on the porch, but it was secure. I went inside to get a plastic bag for all the broken glass. I almost wanted to cry.

After I had picked up all the glass, I went to the swing and picked up my drink. I took another big swig and headed inside to refill it. As I threw the glass in the trash bag, I decided I would bike into town tomorrow and get another feeder. I needed to take care of my hummingbirds.

Just as I was heading out of the kitchen, I heard the door open. Hannah was back. "Hey, Melissa! I can't wait to show you what I got today." Seeing me, she asked, "Are you okay? What happened?" Her mind immediately went to Danny.

Her fear brought me back to reality. It was only a bird feeder. There were bigger concerns right now. "Oh, it's nothing bad. Just somehow, my hummingbird feeder got broken. It's stupid, but it was the first thing I got when I came here. It just makes me kind of sad. It's fine. I'm going to get a new one tomorrow." Changing the subject before I started to cry, I tried to act excited. "Now show me what you bought."

Grabbing the bags, Hannah rushed back into the kitchen and threw her bags on the table. Opening them up, she pulled out outfit after outfit. She was so excited. She even bought new makeup. "I haven't had new makeup in years." She was so happy. As she showed me each new item, I thought to myself, *This is the Hannah Chris has always known. She might have been broken, but she is going to come back stronger, happier, and more confident in herself.*

"How about we cook some hot dogs on the firepit for dinner tonight. We can have chili dogs."

"That sounds great." Hannah headed upstairs to take care of her clothes. I headed outside to start the fire.

Walking in back, I saw the plastic chairs were spread all around the backyard. I had no idea that the wind was so strong. That must have been how my hummingbird feeder got broken. I was glad the wind had stopped so I could start the fire. Crumbling up the newspaper, I stuffed it at the bottom of the firepit and loaded some logs on top of it. Using a match, I lit the paper. The flame quickly died out. Shoving more paper in, I lit it again. Again, the flame went out.

Hannah came out and started laughing. "What are you doing? Haven't you ever started a fire before?"

"Well not a campfire, but how hard can it be? I mean I've lit scented candles before." I tried to make a joke, realizing that it was a lot harder than I thought.

"You have to leave room for air." She took out all the logs that I had piled up. "Go look for little twigs. You need to start small and build your way up." I walked around the yard and picked up a bunch of broken sticks. I also picked up both the chairs that had blown into the yard. I felt a little bit like Lilly, looking for marshmallow sticks.

Handing the twigs to Hannah, she formed them into a teepee and put some paper at the bottom. Lighting it, she said, "As this gets going, you just keep adding more and more sticks. Once you have a good bed of coals going, then you can add in some of the logs."

"Or I could just sit here and watch as you get it going." I sat down in one of the plastic chairs I had just picked up. I watched as she added more and more sticks and eventually leaned two logs together on top of the fire. When they started to burn, they collapsed, and the fire grew. She threw on a couple more logs.

As we sat by the fire, she told me all about the day. "It was so great catching up with old friends today. I hate to sound terrible, but I was a bit relieved to hear their lives weren't perfect either. Of course, their troubles seem way more normal. One of my friends is recently divorced. The other one works a job that she hates. It was so nice not to be the one talking about how terrible my life is. Speaking of which, I made the mistake and listened to the voicemail Danny left me. I played it for my friends so they could hear what I have to deal with. It was terrible, worse than ever."

"Let me hear it." I didn't really want to, but I thought it was important to see what we might be dealing with.

Hannah pulled out her phone and clicked on the speaker button. As she clicked on the voicemail, I said, "Turn it all the way up so I can hear it."

Holding the phone toward me, she clicked play. "I got your divorce papers today, you stupid bitch." His voice was slurred, obviously drunk. "If you think I am signing these, you're crazy. If you ever think your ugly, fat ass will ever get anyone as good as me, you're wrong. Good luck spending the rest of your life living with your loser brother. I don't know why I ever wanted your poor ass anyway. Probably because you were an easy lay. You stupid whore." He went on in a drunken rage. "We can deal with this in person. I'll see you real soon."

My mouth hung open in shock. My hands were actually shaking with anger and fear. "Don't look so surprised, Melissa. This is what I have dealt with for the past couple years. It doesn't even faze me anymore."

"We need to tell Chris and call the police. Doesn't your restraining order prevent him from having contact with you?"

"Yeah, but you know the police can't do anything unless he shows up here." I knew she was probably right, but I was going to tell

Chris anyway. He would go crazy, but it was important that he knew. "Can we not talk about this anymore? I'm tired of it."

I shook my head yes and went inside to get the hot dogs. I started a pot of chili on the stove and texted Chris. "I just heard a crazy, drunken message Danny left Hannah. It was terrible. I am worried about her. Don't say anything to her. I don't want her to know I told you. I just thought you should know." After the chili was set, I headed outside with the hot dogs, buns, and all the condiments.

Setting everything on the table, I said, "I started the chili."

Hannah looked at me upset. "You texted Chris?"

My heart sank. "I'm sorry, Hannah. I am just so afraid that Danny is going to come here and hurt you." I felt as if I betrayed her. "Please don't be mad. I knew if I didn't tell Chris and something happened, he would never forgive me. I'm sorry."

"It's fine. I am just tired of Danny. I am also tired of Chris thinking he is my personal bodyguard. I just want this to be over." Her eyes were filled with tears.

"I'm sorry. I didn't mean to make it worse." Now we were both crying.

"It's fine." She shrugged it off, sticking a hot dog on one of the sticks Chris had sharpened. "Let's just pretend this is Danny's wiener. It will make us feel better." We laughed. "Now go check the chili and bring me a large margarita."

"Will do." I headed inside and stirred the chili. I knew I shouldn't, but I texted Chris again. "I told you about Danny in confidence. I didn't tell you so you would call her." I was pissed. I felt as if he had broken my trust. He immediately called me, and I clicked it to voicemail. I didn't want to deal with this anymore tonight. Looking through the cupboards, I found the biggest cup there was. I filled it for Hannah and refilled my cup from earlier. Heading outside with the glasses, I handed her her cup. Then I ran back inside to get the chili.

We spent the rest of the evening just sitting by the fire and talking. We didn't talk about Danny again although it was always on my mind. Chris had called a few more times, but I had turned off the sound so Hannah would know. After cleaning up, I went upstairs to take a shower. I realized that I really found it relaxing to sit by a fire, but I hated the smell of fire in my hair. As I lay in bed, I listened to Chris's voicemail. He was just as pissed as I was that I didn't expect him to say something to Hannah. I think we both probably had good points. He had been dealing with this for a lot longer than I had. I would call him in the morning. Looking at the shotgun, I went over Chris's instructions again, "safety off, point, and pull."

Chapter 29

I woke up early the next morning and made a big pot of coffee. I knew the scent would probably wake up Hannah, but I still tiptoed around. I hoped she would sleep in as long as possible so I could call my mom and talk to her alone. I poured myself a cup and headed out to the porch swing.

"Hey, Mom," I said as she answered. This was the first time since I had left that I really felt as though I wanted her with me.

"Are you okay, Melissa? You sound depressed." My mom knew me as much as I knew myself.

"I'm okay. I guess I'm just missing you." I told her all about Hannah and Danny, probably more than I should have. I didn't want her to worry, but I also needed someone to talk to who wouldn't yell at me or make me feel bad.

"That sounds scary, Melissa. You know, there is nothing you can really do to help her. It sounds like she is doing everything she can right now. Tell her to be safe. I think I have read that once an abuser finds out that he can no longer be in control of the situation, that is the most dangerous time." Her words scared me.

"Yeah, that is what I'm afraid of. Luckily Danny doesn't know where she is staying. Chris took her car to the auto place where I got my truck fixed. That way, he wouldn't be able to find her. Anyway, I just wanted to vent to you. I miss you. How is your job going?"

She told me all about the mission store. I felt as though I knew the women by how she described them. "Mary complains all the time. We get backed up at the cash register, and suddenly she needs to go get more bags or take the hangers to the back room. Plus, she always complains about her back and insists on sitting down between customers. Ellen is pretty funny though. People come in and want a discount on an item that probably only costs a dollar, and she won't give it to them. She will literally brutalize them verbally. She acts like she is the one that is losing the money. I would just give it to them. I mean who cares." It was so great to talk to her again. When I hung up, I felt so much better. Looking up to where the feeder used to hang, I shook my head. After work, I was going to the hardware store to buy a new feeder.

Work went by slowly. When I was done, I went home to see if Hannah wanted to run with me into town. She said that Chris was going to stop by in the late morning to take her to the police station to file a report on Danny's threatening phone call. "Okay," I said. "If you would rather go alone or if you just want to run out, just take my truck. I'm going to bike into town, so I'll leave the keys on the counter." She was super appreciative. I think she wanted to start handling things on her own. Danny had controlled so much of her life for the last few years, and now Chris was always with her. She wanted to prove to Chris and herself that she was strong enough to handle things on her own.

Washing my face, I pulled my hair up in a bun. I loved the way the wind felt on my back when I was biking. Grabbing my sunglasses, I headed out to the bike. It had been a few days since I took a bike ride, and I was feeling as though I needed the exercise. As I rode past Chris's house, I saw him on the tractor. When he saw me, he waved. I waved back but decided not to stop. I would probably see him this afternoon when he dropped Hannah back off at the house.

Pulling up to the hardware store, I looked up to see if Cyndee's open sign was on. Even though I couldn't see in, I waved, assuming she was cutting someone's hair. Walking in the store, Ruger was in his usual spot, baking in the sun. He opened his eyes, and his tail began to wag although he didn't get up. I wished I had brought him one of my leftover hot dogs. "Hey, Ruger. How's my good boy?" His tail started wagging faster, and he stood up, slowly moseying over to me. I crouched down, and he laid his head on my knee. Scratching behind his ears, I lowered down and put my forehead on his. "You're such a good doggie. Thanks for keeping Betty safe." He licked my face as if he knew what I had said. Standing up, I spotted Betty down the paint aisle.

"Hi, Betty." I waved and headed directly to the bird feeders. I couldn't find the exact feeder I had bought before, but there was another pretty red one that had bright yellow flowers around the bottom. I thought the birds would like that one.

"Adding more feeders to your collection?" she asked. "You're not turning into a crazy bird lady now, are you?"

"No, something happened to my old feeder, and it broke to smithereens." I gave her a huge frown.

"Oh, I'm sorry." She knew how much I loved it.

"I don't know what happened. I think the wind caught it or maybe a big bird knocked it off the hook." I shrugged my shoulders, letting her know that I really had no idea what happened.

"Well I think that feeder is a good one." She pointed to one that was very similar to the one I had. "Do you need any more syrup or corn for the squirrels?" She definitely knew how to upsell.

"Nope, I just want to make sure I get this up before my birds find a better place to get their dinner. I'm going to go up and say hi to Cyndee real quick. Would you mind just holding this at the counter for me until I come back down?"

"Will do," she said, as I headed upstairs. Ruger's eyes followed me all the way. He was back lying in his favorite spot.

As I reached the top of the stairs, I could hear Lilly talking even through the closed door. It always seemed to me that kids had one level of speaking, like a high-pitched yell. "Hey, girlie," I said to Lilly as she launched into my arms and gave me a big hug. Another girl was with her playing dolls, the toy chest was empty, and toys covered the entire floor. "Who's your friend?"

"Cora. That's her mommy." She pointed at the woman getting her hair cut by Cyndee.

"Hey, Melissa," Cyndee yelled across the room. The woman in her chair smiled. "I have about ten more minutes here if you don't mind waiting."

"She can play with us." Lilly was thrilled—me, not so much. I liked kids well enough but definitely knew I wasn't ready to have one any time soon. Before I knew it, I was holding a teacup. Lilly was pouring me coffee, and Cora was bringing me a plastic pork chop on a plate. For the next ten minutes, Lilly must have poured me fifteen cups of coffee. Cora kept taking my plate and bringing me other types of food. I would drink and eat and talk about what a great restaurant it was. They were having the time of their lives. It felt like the longest ten minutes of my life. As Cora's mom came over, she begged her to stay. I was so relieved when she convinced her that they would be back real soon.

As they left, Cyndee sat on the couch next to me. "Start cleaning up now, Lilly." Without an argument, Lilly got right to cleaning up. I was impressed that there wasn't any whining. "How's everything going?"

I told her all about shooting with Chris and the voicemail Danny had left Hannah. "It was super scary. He was so drunk. He was calling her all kinds of names and saying he wouldn't sign the divorce papers. Then he said they could talk about it face-to-face. I made the mistake of telling Chris about it. He called Hannah, and she got all upset with me. I'm kind of in the middle. Chris wants to know every little detail. Hannah wants to deal with it on her own. It's stressful. Chris was going to pick her up today and head to the police station. I guess it's a violation of the PPO for Danny to even be calling Hannah."

"So are they going to arrest him? What's going to happen?"

"I have no idea. I think it's complicated because he lives in another state. If he comes up here, then they can arrest him, but no one wants him to come up here."

"Does Danny know she is staying with you?" She seemed concerned for me.

"I don't think Danny even knows I exist. That is the good thing. I assume he thinks she is staying with her brother. They took her car to Pete's to kind of hide it. So if he does come into town and drives around looking for her car, he won't be able to find it."

"Good thinking. I was going to ask her if she wanted to stay with me, but I can't risk anything happening to Lilly." Suddenly we heard Ruger growling downstairs. Cyndee and I jumped up and tried to look downstairs to see what was going on. I had never heard Ruger upset.

"Ruger is barking, Mom," Lilly announced. "Why is Ruger barking?"

"I don't know. I think I will go look. You stay up here."

"I'll go with you," I said, and we headed down the stairs. Ruger was standing by the door, barking. His hair was standing up at the base of his neck. I looked over at Betty, who was coming up from the back of the store. "What's going on?" I asked. "Ruger's hair is standing up on his neck." Apparently he was a guard dog.

"I'm not sure. I heard the door open and saw a man come in. I yelled that I would be right up, but I couldn't recognize him from way in the back. Ruger likes almost everyone, but something about him made him lose it. Next thing I knew, Ruger was growling and barking. He had scared him right out of the store. It's okay now," she said. "Good boy." She reached down to pet him. "You know, sometimes during the week, we get drunks that come in from the bar. Ruger usually lets us know right away if it is someone of questionable character. More than once, he has been a better judge of character than me. I never worry about losing a sale. What I do worry about is getting robbed by some carny construction worker that is looking to overpower an old woman."

"Oh my gosh. You know, Connie told me that excitement seems to follow me around. I'm starting to think she is right."

"Oh, ignore Connie. She probably loves all the excitement you have brought to town. I am sure she has been bored sick from gossiping about the same old stuff for the past six years." Betty nodded her head toward Cyndee. Cyndee shook her head in agreement.

"I'm just glad she's talking about you now. I was getting tired of being the topic of conversation."

"I'm so glad I could help. You might as well ring me up now," I said, looking at Betty. "I'll catch you later, Cyndee. Tell Lilly thanks for all the coffee."

"Will do." Cyndee went to the popcorn machine and grabbed a bag for her and Lilly. "Look, I just made Lilly lunch." She laughed and headed up the stairs. She teased about being a bad mom, but Lilly was a fantastic young girl.

I thanked Betty and headed out to my bike. No wonder Ruger was upset. I found my bike lying on its side. That stupid drunk must have knocked it over. Picking it up, I looked it over for scratches. It seemed to be okay. I decided to load the feeder into the basket and head straight home. I wanted to make sure I hung it back up before the birds came to feed.

I was filling the feeder with syrup when Hannah and Chris pulled up. Hannah whipped past in a hurry. "I have to pee so bad I almost wet my pants." Chris was following behind.

As I finished filling up the feeder, Chris sat on the steps. When I was done hanging it on the hook, I went and sat next to him. "You still mad at me?" he asked without looking at me.

"No. You still mad at me?" I scooted closer to him.

"No. I was just upset about the whole situation." He put his arm around my shoulder and pulled me closer.

"I know. How'd it go today?" I laid my head on his shoulder and took in a deep breath. The way he smelled was intoxicating.

"They took the report and were going to call the county where he lives so they can deal with him."

Just then, Hannah came back out with the leftover Good and Plenty's. "Have you two lovebirds made up yet?" We smiled. "Grabbed your candy." She held up the bag to show me. "I am starving, and Chris wouldn't get me any food."

"Did you get a new bird feeder?" Chris asked, looking to see what I had hung up.

"Yeah. When I came home the other day. The other one was broken. I was lying in the grass. I think the wind must have blown it off the hook."

"When was it that windy here?" Chris looked at me inquisitively.

"I don't know, but it also blew the chairs across the lawn in the back." I explained how I had to pick them up last night when we were cooking the hot dogs.

"Weird" was all Chris said.

"Not to change the subject, but have you ever heard Ruger bark at anyone before? When I was talking to Cyndee today at her shop, he growled and barked so loudly at a customer that he just left. Cyndee and I ran downstairs to see what was happening, but the guy was already gone. Kathy was in the back and couldn't tell who it was. She said it was probably some drunk from The Brown Trout."

"Nope, never heard him do that before," Chris said. "But he was doing what he was trained to do. Dogs are usually pretty good at reading people."

"That's what Betty said. It was so funny. She said it was probably some carny construction worker." We laughed. "Why don't you guys come in and I'll make us some dinner?"

We all headed inside, and I grabbed some hamburger from the refrigerator. "Does tacos sound okay?" They both agreed, so I put the burger on the stove and started browning it. I grabbed the lettuce and tomatoes. Hannah sat down at the table, so I grabbed a couple of knives and cutting boards. She and I started cutting. Chris was leaning against the sink, looking out the back door.

"I'll be right back," he said and headed outside.

"What's he doing?" I asked Hannah.

"Who knows. He is probably just getting some fresh air. He gets so angry having to deal with Danny's BS." I got up to grab a couple of bowls to put the lettuce and tomatoes in. I looked out the back door and watched as Chris walked around the house, looking at the dirt and under all the windows.

When he walked back in, he didn't say anything. "You know we have actual toilets in this house. If you have to pee, you don't need to go outside."

"Very funny," he said, grabbing a wooden spoon and spanking my butt before using it to stir the meat. "This is about done. Do you have any seasoning?" He started opening cupboards.

"It's in the cupboard next above the sink." I pointed.

He grabbed the pan and drained the grease from the burger into an old can that was in the recycle bin. Then he grabbed a small glass, filled it with water and poured it over the meat, and added the seasoning on top. He stirred it, put the lid on the pan, then turned down the heat. Then he went over to the drawer and grabbed some silverware to set the table. "As soon as you have everything cut up, the meat will be ready."

Standing up, I grabbed the cheese, salsa, and tortilla shells out of the refrigerator and put them on the table. Hannah grabbed three paper plates from the top of the microwave and put them on the table. "Looks like we are all set. Can you just grab a couple spoons and a big one for the meat?" I asked Hannah. Chris grabbed a hot pad, then brought over the meat, and set it on the table.

As we sat down, I asked, "Do you mind if I just say grace?" Chris took off his hat, and we all bowed our heads. I just said something simple, but I felt as though I needed to pray. When I was done, I said, "I think I am going to head to church tomorrow morning. I haven't gone since I got here, and I feel like it's something I am missing. Is there a church in town?" Hannah told me about the nondenominational church, the Baptist, and the Catholic churches. The nondenominational church had a 9:00 a.m. service, so I decided to go there. I thought I might try the other churches some other weekends to see which one I felt most comfortable at. I was raised Catholic, so I knew I would understand what was going on there. Hannah said the nondenominational church served espresso and cookies, and I thought that sounded amazing. I had no idea what went on at the Baptist Church, but I was willing to give anything a shot once.

"Do you guys have any plans for tomorrow?" I looked at Chris and then Hannah.

"I'm just going to work around the farm in the morning. Why don't you stop over on your way home from Church?"

"Sounds good. What about you, Hannah?" I asked, still worried about leaving her alone.

"Kathy is going to pick me up around eleven. We are going to go to a few open houses. She found a couple little two-bedroom houses that are for sale right out of town. I think I need to start planning what I am going to do next. I mean I love staying here, but I want to see what's out there. I also want to start looking for a job. I have been secretly stashing money away for the last year, but that money isn't going to last very long."

I tried to avoid talking about this, but I knew I had to, "Maybe you could just rent this place after I leave." Chris looked at me and locked eyes with me. Looking away, I continued, "I need to start looking for a job too. I love it here more than I could have ever imagined, but I am going to have to get back to reality soon. I barely make enough at the bakery to pay for groceries, and my money is running out." Chris still didn't say anything. He just continued to stare at me. I couldn't tell if he was mad at me or just very serious.

"You can't leave me now. I need you." Hannah got up and gave me a hug from behind my chair. "I'll be right back. I think I better call Kathy to make sure we are still on for tomorrow."

"Aren't you going to say anything?" I looked at Chris.

"What do you want me to say?" Now I could tell he was mad.

"I don't know, but say something. Tell me what you are thinking." I stood up and walked behind him and hugged him around the back of his chair.

"You know what I'm thinking, Mel." He stood up to break out of my hug and walked over to throw his paper plate in the garbage. Then he started clearing the table, throwing the silverware in the sink.

"I never planned on staying here all summer. I mean if you hadn't helped me, I wouldn't even be here right now." Chris continued clearing the table, not acknowledging my conversation. "I really care about you, Chris. I mean, I need to know what you are thinking." I really just wanted to hear him tell me how much he liked me, that I was more than just a summer fling, that maybe there could be a future for us. "Do you want me to stay? Are you okay with me leaving? I need to know."

"We'll if you need to go back, I'm not going to ask you to stay. You know how I feel about you, but I can't ask you to stay here with me. That has to be a decision you make on your own. I don't want to be the one that gets blamed if things don't work out."

It was my turn now just to look at him. *Really*, I thought. *He doesn't want to be the one who gets blamed if it doesn't work out between the two of us.* He really had no clue how to deal with women. All I wanted was for him to ask me to stay, to tell me he couldn't imagine his life without me, to tell me that he might not know where our relationship is going, but he was willing to risk finding out. But nope, I wasn't worth the risk. He was willing to just let me go. That told me a lot.

"Yep, we're still on," Hannah said, busting into the kitchen and breaking my train of thought. "What's going on?" She looked at Chris and then at me.

"Nothing," said Chris. "I better head out though. I still have to get some stuff done before tomorrow."

Hannah looked at me, but I avoided eye contact. It was my turn now to finish cleaning up the table. Chris said goodbye and started toward the front door, and Hannah followed behind him. I could hear Hannah from the other room, "Geez, Chris, you better get it together, or she is going to leave. She makes you happier than I have ever seen you, and you're just going to mess it all up."

"You have your own problems to worry about, Hannah. Just worry about yourself." I hadn't heard him speak to her like this before.

"Oh you're one to talk." Her voice got louder. "You keep trying to fix my life, but you can't even handle your own." Chris left, the door slamming behind him.

"You can't leave, Melissa." She walked over to the sink and spoke directly to my face. "Chris loves you. He is just afraid to tell you. And you know you love him too. I see it the way you two look at each other. Have you told him yet?" I shook my head. "Well he's not going to tell you first, I can guarantee that. After the mess with Cyndee, he won't risk getting hurt like that again. He just wants to know that you think he's worth staying. He needs to know that you won't just walk out on him."

"I just wanted him to ask me to stay. I didn't expect for him to tell me he loves me. All he had to do was ask me to stay."

"Well he's never going to do that. So if you're leaving, stop messing with his heart. I don't have it in me to see him retreat back into the old, reclusive Chris. He deserves to be happy. So maybe you just need to decide. If you are going to leave, leave so that he can move on. Because I am the one that will be here having to deal with him." She stomped away and headed outside.

I could hear the porch swing creaking as she rocked back and forth. I continued to finish up in the kitchen. I thought about what Hannah had said and knew she was right. I did love Chris. I didn't want to leave. This was all very scary.

Grabbing a couple of glasses, I filled them up with margaritas and headed out to the porch. "I come bearing gifts." I handed her a margarita and sat next to her.

"You two are idiots." She laughed and leaned into me on the swing.

"I know," I responded.

Chapter 30

Getting up early, I looked through my clothes to decide what to wear. I had never been to a nondenominational church. I had no idea if they dressed up or wore something casual. It was always weird going into a new church. I just wanted to make sure I didn't stand out. I decided on a light sundress with sunflowers on it. I was glad I was going. I felt as if my life was a whirlwind lately and looked forward to getting a little peace and time to refocus.

Driving up, I could see that the building was an active warehouse, converted into a church on Sundays. The parking lot was packed. People were getting out of their cars dressed in shorts and T-shirts. Others were wearing dress pants and ties and dresses. I think it was pretty much a come-as-you-are kind of church. I followed the crowd to the front door.

Walking up, a young man and a woman each held a door open. They greeted me as I entered the door. Inside, there was a tall table and an older woman standing behind it. "Welcome," she said. "Have you been here before?" Apparently it was obvious that I hadn't. I smiled, and she walked over to me. "Well welcome. Let me show you where you need to go. Do you want some coffee and a cookie?"

"A coffee would be great." She led me over to a table packed with cookies, coffee, tea, and bottles of water.

"Just grab whatever you want and head over and sit down anywhere you are comfortable." Smiling, she returned to her post.

I thanked her and headed toward a large open room that was filled with rows of folding chairs. A large movie screen was pulled down. In front of the screen, drums, keyboards, and guitars were set up. This was not like any other church I had ever been to. Right before 9 a.m., a group of younger adults grabbed their instruments and started playing Christian music at a noise level that I had never heard in a church before. Verses for the songs played across the movie screen, just in case you didn't know the words. Everyone was standing up and singing. Some waved their hands in front of them. As I stood up, I drank my coffee and took it all in. I had to admit that it was a little more progressive than I was used to.

After a few songs, the pastor came out. He was a lot younger than any pastor I had ever had. He was tall and clean-cut, dressed in jeans and a polo shirt. The topic for the service was trusting in the Lord. As he preached, I was drawn into his words. He spoke eloquently and with humor. I could tell he was well versed in the bible but preached in a way that was easily relatable. As he spoke, I thought about my life. I did just have to trust in the Lord, especially when it came to Chris and me. I prayed the best thing would happen.

Before I knew it, I was heading back to my truck. I sat in the parking lot for a second and watched as everyone came out to their vehicles. I was shocked at the number of people that attended. They must have come from way out of town. Instead of just jumping in their cars and racing away, groups formed outside, and everyone stayed around to talk. It definitely was a community church. Although I was a little shocked by the music, I didn't rule out coming back. It did have a good message.

Before pulling out, I decided to call Chris. "Hey, Mel," he answered. I liked the sound of his voice. Something about it made my stomach churn nervously.

"Are you still planning on me coming over?" I wasn't really sure after our argument.

"Yes," he responded. He was a man of few words.

"Great. I just got out of church. I am going to head downtown and pick up a few things for lunch. I'll head over when I'm done. Give me about forty-five minutes."

"Sounds good. Umm, Mel," he continued hesitantly. "I don't want you to leave." I was quiet for a second. "Are you still there?"

I didn't know what to say. Hannah had told me he would never tell me to stay. This was more than I thought I would ever hear from him. "Yeah, I'm still here. I don't want to leave either." I could almost hear him sigh with relief. "We'll talk more when I get to your house, okay."

"Okay." He hung up the phone. He was a man of few words. But today, he said just what I needed to hear.

Chapter 31

As I drove up to the grocery store, I was still gathering my wallet and list when Connie ran out and knocked on the passenger window. Her face was panicked. "What's up, Connie? Everything okay?"

"Where's Hannah?" She was speaking fast.

"She is out with Kathy. What's up?"

"Danny was just in here buying beer. He was super drunk and acting crazy. I am worried about what he might do." By this point, she was almost yelling.

I didn't even thank her. I started up my truck and raced toward Chris's house. As I pulled in, he was standing near the barn. "That was fast," he said as he came toward my truck.

Jumping out, I almost yelled, "Danny."

"What's going on? What about Danny?" He grabbed me by the shoulders, trying to get me to focus.

"I just went to the grocery store, and Connie didn't even let me get out of the truck. She said he was in the store buying booze and that he was super drunk and acting weird. Have you heard from Kathy and Hannah?" My whole body was shaking.

"Let's go," he yelled. Chris jumped into the driver's side of my truck, and I got in the passenger side. I wasn't even buckled up before he was speeding out of the driveway. "Call Hannah," he yelled.

I picked up the phone. My hands were shaking as I called her. It rang and rang. "Pick up," I whispered. "Pick up."

"Try Kathy." He continued driving toward the farmhouse. Kathy didn't pick up either. Still there was no answer. Chris almost parked on top of the front porch as he jumped out and ran inside. Coming right back, he yelled, "She's not here."

He jumped back into the truck, and we raced toward Kathy's house. I continued to call Hannah and Kathy; neither were answering. Pulling into her drive, again, Chris jumped out and ran to the door. Turning around, he looked at me and shook his head. Coming back to the truck, he said, "They aren't here either. Do you know where the houses are that they were going to look at?"

"I don't. I just know that it was in town somewhere. What do you want to do? Do you want to head over to Danny's parents' house to see if he's there?" Just then, Hannah picked up the phone.

"Oh my gosh, Hannah. I have been trying to get a hold of you." I didn't mean to, but I was screaming at her.

"We're walking through houses. What's up?" She was not ready for the answer.

Chris took the phone. "Danny is here."

"What do you mean? Where is he? Is he with you?" She was confused and stressed.

"No, he was in town this morning. Mel went to the store, and Connie told her that he was there this morning. I guess he was really drunk and acting crazy. It was so bad that Connie was afraid for you." I could hear Kathy in the background asking what was happening. "Don't go home yet. Melissa and I are going to head out to his parents' house to see if he is there. I will call you and let you know what is going on."

We drove toward the lakeshore in silence. Chris's eyes were red with rage. I was worried about what he might do if Danny was there. As we pulled into their driveway, Chris jumped out of the truck. "Stay here," he ordered. I did what he told me to, but I rolled down the windows so I could hear what was going on.

As he knocked on the door, I looked at the white construction truck in the driveway. It was the same truck that had been at The Brown Trout lot earlier in the week.

An older short man answered the door. Seeing that it was Chris, he came outside and shut the door behind him. I wondered if he was trying to hide Danny inside. I could hear Chris yelling about Danny, the restraining order, and the divorce. The man yelled back, "He isn't here, and he hasn't been here." He stepped closer to Chris, trying to intimidate him. His small stature was no match for Chris. As he yelled for Chris to get the hell off his property, I watched to see what Chris would do.

As Chris came back to the truck, he turned around and warned the man, "You better tell him not to go anywhere near Hannah, or I will end him."

Chris got back in the truck, and we peeled away. "Can you just text Hannah that Danny wasn't at his parents' house? Let's drive into town and see if we can spot him." I didn't think that was a good idea, but I didn't say anything.

Driving down the main street, Chris drove in front of and behind all the stores. Then he stopped at the grocery store to speak with Connie. She was outside smoking. I think the stress was more than she could take. I watched through the truck window as he spoke with Connie. She was waving her arms up and down and pointing as she spoke. I could tell it really upset her. As much of a busy body and gossip as she was, she did genuinely care about Hannah and Chris. I might have misjudged her, I thought. She hugged Chris as she headed back inside the store.

As he got into the truck, he said, "Let's head back to your farmhouse and wait for Hannah and Kathy. Can you ask them to meet us there?"

I texted them and told them we were headed home. "At least, Danny doesn't know about me. He won't know to look for Hannah there."

Chris looked at me and shook his head. "I'm not sure he doesn't know."

"What do you mean?" I was confused.

"The other day when your bird feeder was broken and the lawn chairs were spread across the lawn, I checked the weather for those days. It wasn't windy." Leave it to Chris to research the weather that day. "When I went outside yesterday, I checked around and didn't see any footprints, but I'm still not convinced it wasn't him."

"I recognized the truck in Danny's parents' driveway." My voice started to shake.

"What do you mean you recognized it? Was it at your house? Did you see him drive by?" He was yelling again, although not at me but more toward me.

"No, that was one of the trucks that was at The Brown Trout the other day when I drove by. I'm not saying it was Danny, but if he was driving his dad's work truck, he might have been at the bar."

"I wouldn't doubt it." His eyes glared, deepening the crease between his eyes.

"Do you want to stop in there and ask?" I didn't know if that was a good idea or not.

"No, it doesn't matter now. He has probably been in town for a few days, hiding out at his parents' house. We need to get to your place, so we're there if he shows up."

"Do you think it could have been Danny that showed up at the hardware store? You know, the guy the Ruger barked at." My mind instantly went to the worst-case scenario. "You don't think he was going there to get ammunition, do you?"

Chris looked at me. "We just need to get to your place."

Chapter 32

As we drove in, Kathy pulled in behind us. It looked like Hannah had been crying. We all stood in the driveway and tried to decide what to do. We suggested that Kathy go home. We wanted few people around just in case something did happen.

"We need to call the police," I suggested. "They need to know that he is in town." We walked toward the house and went inside. Chris stayed out on the front porch to call the police. Hannah and I went in and sat down at the kitchen table.

"How are you holding up?" I asked, but I could tell she was about to lose it.

"I'm fine. I am just hoping he doesn't find out where I am at. I just don't want to have to deal with him." I didn't want to tell her about what Chris had said about the hummingbird feeder and the lawn chairs. We didn't know if that was actually Danny, and I didn't want to make her any more upset.

Chris came into the kitchen and widened his eyes at me, behind Hannah's back. "Well now the police know. They said it's not illegal for him to be in town. He can be anywhere he wants to be as long as it's away from you. So unless he tries something, there is nothing they can do."

"That is ridiculous," I yelled. "So unless he tries to hurt her, they can't do anything? What is the point of a restraining order then?" I was furious.

"It's just how it works." Chris was leaning against the sink. "I think you guys need to stay here today until we can figure things out."

"I'm not going to hide from him, Chris. I spent the last few years afraid to say or do anything that might make him mad. I was always afraid of what he might do. I am not going to live in fear anymore."

"I understand, but let's not risk things right now. I will stay here with you guys just in case." He calmed himself down. "Please, Hannah."

"You are not going to babysit me. I'm not doing that. Melissa is here. We can hang out here today, but I'm not locking myself inside." She was very matter-of-fact. "Now go, leave. You have farmwork to do. We will call you if we need you. You literally live three minutes away. I am sure you can make it over here in time if something happens."

I looked at Chris, not sure what to say. "We can just stay here and maybe look at more houses on Zillow or check to see if there are any job openings listed online. You know, for both of us." I tried to change the mood.

Hannah's head flew up. "So you're staying?" Chris stared at me. "Well we haven't really talked about it yet, but I'm going to need a job."

She came over and hugged me. I could see Chris's face relax a little. "Alright, I'll leave, but I'm not going far. Call me if Danny shows up."

After he left, I sat at the table with Hannah. "Want some coffee?" I thought a drink was more appropriate, but coffee was probably the smarter option.

"Please. My nerves are shot, and I need something to calm me down. Is it too early for a wine cooler?" She was thinking the same thing.

"In this case, probably not, but if we are going to look for a job, we should probably stick to coffee." I made coffee and sat down at the table. "Are you doing okay?"

"I'm not really sure. I am kind of just numb." I could see the stress on her face.

"Do you think he will try to find you?" I asked hesitantly, hoping she would say no.

"Oh, he is looking for me. I don't want to have to deal with this. I am afraid Chris will do something stupid and end up in jail."

Getting up, I poured both of us a cup of coffee. "How about if we split a can of chicken noodle soup? I think it will be good to eat something. The only thing I had to eat all morning was cookies at church."

"Oh, how was it? I have never been there before. I've heard good things."

"The message was good. It was very progressive. They had a rock band playing Christian music and a movie screen. Everyone was singing, and people were raising their hands. I asked the lady in front of me with her hand raised if she had a question."

"What? You did not!" Hannah's mouth dropped open.

"No, I'm just kidding." Hannah laughed with relief. "The pastor was super young and dressed in jeans. He was really good. I'm just not sure I can get used to the music. I will probably go to the Catholic Church next. I might go back there sometime though." I opened the can of soup and poured it into a pan. Hannah went upstairs to grab her computer.

Setting the computer on the table, she said, "Do you want to see the houses Kathy and I looked at this morning? We didn't really get much time in the second one, but they were both pretty nice."

As she showed me, her phone began to buzz. "Oh no, that isn't Danny, is it?"

"No, it's a text from Chris. He's coming over." Our relaxed mood went into high stress as soon as she read the text. "Something must be up."

I turned off the soup, and we headed outside. Chris came flying into the driveway and pulled up to the porch. "Pete just called. Your windows have been broken out of your car. The police are at his shop. Let's go."

"What? Seriously. It had to be Danny." Hannah was in a full panic. As Chris pulled into Pete's, two police cars were parked out back by Hannah's car. Pete and Kathy were talking with them as they took notes. Chris pulled right up next to the cop cars.

Hannah jumped out and raced over to her car. All the windows were broken out, and two of the tires were slashed. She began to cry uncontrollably. "I can't take this anymore." She crouched down on the ground. I bent down and tried to lift her up. She seemed so heavy. She couldn't hold in her pain anymore.

"Come on, Hannah." I tried to get her to stand up. "It's going to be okay. Now the police can arrest him. Come on." As she stood up, I walked her over to the truck. "Wait here." I put her inside and walked over to Chris and the police.

Kathy walked past me. "I'll stay out here with Hannah." She went to the truck and sat next to Hannah. I watched as Hannah's head fell on Kathy's shoulder. She seemed so defeated.

As I walked over to Chris, everyone started heading inside. "What's going on?" I was a little confused.

"Pete has surveillance cameras." Chris grabbed my hand, as we headed toward the office. Pete went in first and pulled out an old VHS type. I was a little concerned that it would show anything. The recorder must have been at least twenty years old. The police officers got as close as they could to the TV screen to get a good view. Chris and I packed in behind them.

Pete popped the tape into the player and rewound it to the beginning of the day. Pressing fast forward, Pete stopped the tape as a man approached Hannah's car. The footage was dark and fuzzy. We watched as the man picked up a tire iron from behind the shop. One by one, he smashed the windows. The tape didn't play sound, but we could tell he was screaming. Pulling a knife from his pocket, he bent down to slash a tire, falling drunkenly on his side. Pulling himself up, he jabbed the knife into the side of the tire. Then he walked back and slashed the rear tire. As he stood back up, he was facing directly at the camera, "Stop it there," the cop said, pointing at the man on the TV.

Pete paused the tape, and we all looked at the man. "That's Danny," Chris said. "That's him." The officers looked at Pete, who agreed. "Yep, that's him."

"Okay," they said, standing up. "We're going to need that tape." Pete handed them the tape. As we left the office, the officer pulled Chris aside and began to whisper. I couldn't hear what they were saying.

"I'm sorry about this, Melissa." It was the first time since I had met Pete that I could hear his age in his voice. "Please let Hannah know." I could see that he was visibly shaken.

"She knows. Thanks for everything. This has nothing to do with you." As we were walking over to the truck, Kathy got out and walked over to Pete.

"Thanks, Kathy. I'll let you know if we hear anything." We hugged, and Pete and Kathy headed back toward the shop. Chris stopped them and talked for a second. When he reached me, I asked, "What did the police say?"

"They are going to keep an eye on your house tonight to make sure you guys are safe. They think that Danny might show up. They will let us know as soon as they arrest him."

"Okay, good." It wasn't really a relief, but I pretended it was.

Chris demanded, "And I am staying with you guys tonight whether or not Hannah likes it or not." We both got into the truck. Hannah was still crying. "They have footage of Danny," Chris told Hannah. "They are going to find him."

Chapter 33

Chris drove my truck back to his house. "I'm going to take shower and grab a change of clothes. I'll be over as soon as I'm out." We both got out of the truck.

As I walked around the front of the truck, Chris met me. I kissed him and gave him a long hug. "Thanks for taking care of Hannah today. You are her rock."

He squeezed me in tightly. "I'll be over in a few minutes. Go inside and lock the doors."

I got into the driver's seat. Hannah had moved upfront. "You okay?" I asked, knowing that she wasn't. She shook her head yes. I started the truck and headed home. We pulled up next to the house and ran inside, locking the doors behind us.

Once we got inside, I asked Hannah, "Are you ready for the soup now?"

"I don't even know if I can eat. I am so upset." She hadn't stopped crying since she saw her car.

"Well the soup is still on the stove from this morning. Why don't you just start the burner?. Then when Chris comes back, we can all have a little something. I will be in the kitchen in a second."

As I ran upstairs to get the shotgun, I could hear Chris pulling into the driveway. I was glad he was going to be spending the night. I felt way better knowing that if someone needed to use the shotgun, it would be Chris and not me. "Chris is here," I yelled into the kitchen to Hannah. I picked up the gun and headed down the stairway.

"Hey, Chris," I said, swinging the door open. As he looked up, I realized it was Danny walking up the stairs, not Chris. He lunged toward the door, but I was able to slam it tight before he reached it. As I began to scream, Hannah raced out of the kitchen. "Call 911,"

I yelled. "It's Danny." I dead bolted the door but was too scared to step away from it.

"Open up," he yelled. "I just want to talk to Hannah."

"She isn't here," I yelled. "I have a gun. Get off my porch." I was terrified but tried to be demanding.

"Open up this door, or I'm going to break it down," he screamed, as he slammed his body repeatedly against the door. "I just want to talk with her. Open this door," he screamed with rage. "We can work this out, Hannah. Just open the door."

I could hear Hannah screaming on the phone in the kitchen. I prayed the police would be here soon. "Hannah isn't here. I called the police. They are on their way." I held the door tightly. My entire body pressed tightly against it. I worried the dead bolt wouldn't hold up. "If you don't get away from my door, I will shoot you through it." I grabbed the shotgun; my hands were shaking uncontrollably. The pounding stopped at the door. I wanted to go to the window to see if he was leaving, but I didn't dare move from the door. I listened for his car to start up.

As I looked up, Hannah was heading out of the kitchen. "Get back in the kitchen," I screamed. She looked at me terrified and raced back into the kitchen. Holding the gun up, I stepped back and walked toward the window. I was almost to the window when my bike came crashing through the glass. I screamed in terror. He began pulling at the bike, trying to clear a way to enter. He was yanking and yanking. I tried holding onto the front tire, so he wouldn't be able to remove it. Finally, I backed away from the window, holding the gun up. Going over Chris's instructions in my head, I realized I had forgotten to click the safety off. I clicked it off with my thumb, holding the gun toward the window. I was shaking uncontrollably. "I will shoot you." I was done giving warnings.

Suddenly I heard the police from the driveway. "Back away from the window." I didn't lower my gun. Physically, I was frozen with fear.

"I just came here to talk. I'm not leaving. I just want to talk to my wife," he screamed back. He wasn't leaving. I didn't move, holding my aim at the window.

"Come off the porch," they repeated. "We will shoot you."

I took a step closer to the window, crouching down and peaking up between the bike tires. Danny stepped away from the window but stopped at the top of the porch stairs. Facing the police, he screamed again, "I just need to talk to Hannah. Let me talk to her first. I will come down, but I just want to talk to her first." He held his hands in the air as if he was willing to surrender.

"Leave your hands up and turn around. Walk backward toward us." The cops continued to point their guns toward Danny. He wasn't moving. Looking out, I could see three cop cars. One was blocking the driveway. A fire truck was blocking cars from coming down the street. Chris was outside, standing in front of his truck. A cop was physically preventing him from coming up the driveway. I watched as he was struggling to break free.

"I just need to talk to her," Danny yelled. I could feel my fear growing. He wasn't going to leave. "Let me just talk with her." He kept repeating himself. I watched as he began to slowly lower his hands. Reaching behind his back, he lifted his shirt. I saw a gun tucked in his pants.

"He's got a gun," I screamed as loud as I could. Before I knew it, he had pulled the gun and was raising it toward the police. Gunshots rang through the air. It happened so fast I wasn't sure who was shooting. I threw myself to the ground, using my arms to protect my head. Screaming, Hannah ran out of the kitchen toward the door.

Jumping up and running toward her, I threw my body onto hers, knocking her to the ground. "Stop, Hannah. You can't go out there." Screaming and crying on the floor, she tried to break loose. "No, Hannah. You don't want to see this. Please." She continued to scream in agony. I held her tightly as we lay together on the floor. Within seconds, I could hear the police on the porch. Chris came bursting through the door.

Falling to the ground, he grabbed us. "It's over. It's over." I burst into tears, no longer able to hold it in. I let go of Hannah as Chris helped her up. "It's over now," he whispered again to us.

As the police came in, neither of us looked toward the door. We didn't want to see Danny. We knew he was dead.

For the next few hours, the police took our statements. The paramedics came in and bandaged my arms. I hadn't even noticed that they were all cut up from the window glass. Although they wanted to take me to the hospital to get some stitches, I refused to go.

At some point, the coroner came to get Danny's body. When the police finally left, I helped Hannah upstairs to her bed. As she lay down in a ball, I covered her with a quilt. Tears continued to stream down her cheeks, although she wasn't actually crying. I lay with her, rubbing her back until she eventually nodded off.

As I walked down the stairs, I stepped through broken glass, which still covered the floor. I went into the kitchen to grab a broom. As I began to sweep, I saw Chris through the window, spraying the front porch with a hose. I watched as he scrubbed all the blood from the concrete. When I had all the glass cleaned up, I opened the door.

"I'll get some plywood from the barn and cover up the window." He always felt he had to take care of everything.

"Don't worry about that right now. I don't want to wake up Hannah. Do you mind if I come out?" I just needed to be closer to him.

"Please." As I stepped out, he pulled me in and hugged me. "I don't know what I would have done if anything happened to either one of you today." We sat down on the porch swing for a while. "I am sorry I wasn't here for you. I don't know if I will ever be able to forgive myself for not protecting you." I realized he had been as scared as we were.

"Chris, you have done nothing but help me since I first met you." I laid down on the swing, laying my head in his lap.

Rubbing my hair, he asked softly, "You're not going to leave me now, are you? I honestly don't think I could handle it if you left me."

Looking up into his eyes, I said, "I'm not going to leave you." I decided to risk it all. "I can't leave the man I love."

Staring back at me, he grabbed me from under my shoulders and lifted me into a seated position on his lap. I wrapped my arms around his neck. With one hand on my back and the other behind my head, he pulled me in for a hard, deep kiss. Our eyes remained open and locked onto each other's gaze. As our lips released, he took in a deep breath and whispered, "I love you too. I love you too." I knew everything was going to be okay. We were all going to be okay.

125

About the Author

Kim Peterson is an author of sweet romance novels that her mother wouldn't be embarrassed to read.